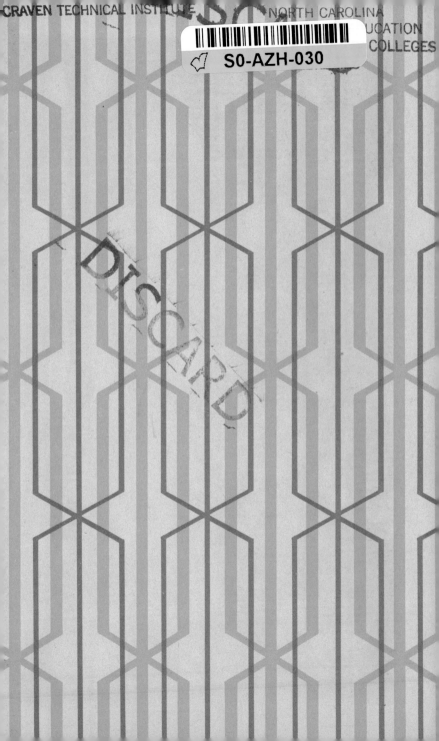

THE DEVIL OF THE WOODS

THE DEVIL
OF THE WOODS

■ A Collection of Thirteen Animal Stories

by PAUL ANNIXTER

Short Story Index Reprint Series

BOOKS FOR LIBRARIES PRESS

 FREEPORT, NEW YORK

STANDARD BOOK NUMBER:
8369-3011-8

LIBRARY OF CONGRESS CATALOG CARD NUMBER:

70-81259

MANUFACTURED
BY
HALLMARK LITHOGRAPHERS, INC.
IN THE U.S.A.

For Jane

ACKNOWLEDGMENTS

To *Country Gentleman Magazine* for "Horns of Plenty," copyright November 1952 by The Curtis Publishing Company and the author.

To *Esquire Magazine* for "Search for the Firebird," copyright February 1946 by Esquire-Coronet, Inc. and the author.

To *Collier's Magazine* for "Trumpeter of the Air Lanes," copyright August 11, 1928 by The Crowell-Collier Com- and the author.

To *Country Gentleman Magazine* for "The Blasted Pine," copyright 1928 by The Curtis Publishing Company and the author.

To *Esquire Magazine* for "The Devil of the Woods," copyright 1945 by Esquire-Coronet, Inc. and the author.

To *Short Story Magazine* for "The Secret Place," copyright 1927 by *Short Story Magazine* and the author.

To *Esquire Magazine* for "The Odyssey of Old Specs," copyright April 1945 by Esquire-Coronet, Inc. and the author.

To *The American Boy Magazine* for "The Keepers of the River Dam," copyright 1928 by The American Boy and the author.

To *Liberty Magazine* for "Deer Slayer," copyright January 1931 by *Liberty Magazine* and the author.

To *The Rod & Gun Magazine* for "Injun Devil," copyright 1929 by *Rod & Gun Magazine* and the author.

To *The Saturday Evening Post*, for "Monarch of the Lagoons," copyright 1929 by The Curtis Publishing Company and the author.

To *Collier's Magazine* for "Flounder, Flounder in the Sea," copyright December 1928 by the Crowell-Collier Publishing Company and the author.

To *Successful Farming Magazine* for "Seekonk, the Tale of a Sea Gull," copyright 1931 by *Successful Farming Magazine* and the author.

CONTENTS

THE DEVIL OF THE WOODS

▪ Horns of Plenty

NAT MARSHALL CREPT FROM HIS BUNK BEFORE DAWN THAT cold February morning and dressed without rousing his wife. He couldn't risk having her argue against his purpose again, for he had made up his mind. In the cabin, Karen's domain, he enjoyed giving way to her, but this matter of Big Eye and his flock had come to involve the very food they would put in their mouths for the coming season, their chance to stay on at the claim. Sentiment must go.

The night before, knowing he was going up the mountain, he had put some biscuit and jerky in his Mackinaw pocket. He would forego coffee and munch on them as he climbed, he thought, gazing out the frosted window at the white-shrouded Shoshone peaks lying tranced and silent as in an interstellar sleep in the faintly growing light.

It was not until he slipped into his Mackinaw that Marshall knew that his wife had been aware that he was going this morning, even though she had said nothing about it. She had wrapped a package of food for him and put it in the deep inner pocket of his coat. A sizable meal it was, heavy and bulkier than he would have wanted, but he would not risk unwrapping it now. It was a token of Karen's forgiveness after their bitter words of yesterday.

1

He laid the note he had written her the night before on the table and took up his loaded rifle. Outside he slipped his arctics into the thongs of his snowshoes and turned his face up the mountain. It had snowed more in the night and got warmer. The cabin on its small terrace was indistinguishable two hundred yards away, one with the mountain's new white anonymity. More snow was predicted for today, according to the radio. It was foolhardy in a way to venture up the mountain, but Nat couldn't face being cabin-bound another day. It was one of those times when the bottom was too close for the Marshalls to risk even silence together.

For two years he and Karen had stuck it out in this lonely cabin on Firetop Mountain. Two years among the high peaks, their only companions the snow that drifted heap on heap all winter, the burning heat of summer, the rare air of the heights that struck the spirit stark awake, much bacon and venison—and a hope. Hope of the wealth that lay beneath the rock formation of Marshall's claim—the treasure that still held him off as it had held off the Delkar brothers who had originally opened up this mine, until they had come out of the mountains, broke and beaten. But Nat came of the tribe of never-give-ups.

In other parts of the world younger men were fighting grim last-ditch battles in foxholes, in shell holes and the cockpits of screaming planes. Nat Marshall was waging his in a hole in a mountainside. And after twenty-six months he had only *begun* to fight.

This was their first unbroken winter on the claim. Only twice in two years had Karen been outside to a town, and no woman was built for that kind of isolation. Her sole release of late had been sitting over their dry-cell radio, straining to catch the occasional musical programs that came over the air when conditions were right. She loved good music and she'd built into him a growing love for it, too, during the empty winter months, before the last battery he had brought in began to peter out. Marshall hated to think of the day it would die completely, leaving them in the unalleviated clamp of the cold, the snow and the silence.

It had seemed such a snug and sensible idea to stay on, back in the fall; much better than Marshall's usual procedure of getting a winter job in some valley town. With a careful buying of necessities they would have enough to see them through until spring. But they had not reckoned with the winter wild. The silence of the heights was more than a silence; it was like a grim categorical presence in which their beings shrunk to hard tight knots in their stand against the great suction of solitude. Almost too much to bear, it had been since the winter storms set in, that deathly diamond stillness. In the midst of it their very dreams had lost life and color and fallen to bits. Of late they had come as close to cabin fever as two people who love can get.

As he plodded upward, Marshall went over again the heated words he'd had with Karen the day before. Their argument, as usual, had revolved about Big Eye, the boss of the band of mountain sheep that roamed the peaks above their cabin. They had talked until Nat had feared further words and had gone out for a tramp in the snow. The wild sheep were friends and neighbors, Karen had maintained, and a man didn't go out and murder neighbors.

"I suppose Old Gray, the Firetop grizzly, is a good neighbor too," he had jeered.

"Of course he is," Karen said. "He's living the life the Lord intended for him here and he's never harmed us. He's got even more right than we have to be here." Her Irish was a fount of such fey and fanciful ideas.

It had gone on and on, for there had been that tempting

offer made to Marshall the fall before by Fraser, the wealthy Denver trophy hunter, whom he had guided on a sheep hunt among the rims. Fraser, who was a hunter of renown and had followed the game trails of three continents, wanted only record heads, and this was one to satisfy his fondest dreams, for Big Eye was a patriarch of his kind. For three years Fraser had known about the magnificent old ram and three times he had tried for his head, but once more, despite a week of stalking and Marshall's intimate knowledge of the heights, Big Eye had been too much for him. Several times it had seemed they had the sheep cornered on some rocky pinnacle from which there was no escape, but each time the boss ram had magicked his followers to safety down some dizzy unguessed stairway of rock on the sheer face of the precipice.

In November, Fraser had given up, chagrined and beaten. Before he left he had said to Marshall: "I still want that ram, Nat. He's something I've got to have and whether my rifle or another man's brings him down doesn't matter any more. There's five hundred in it for you if you get me his head."

That promise, plus the pay he had gotten for guiding, had decided Marshall to winter it on Firetop. Sometime during the winter, he figured, his chance would come to earn that easy money. Five hundred dollars would be a little fortune to him and Karen, enable them to stay on indefinitely, even hire a shovel-stiff to help at the mine in the spring. Karen and the odd whims of chance and weather had held Marshall off so far, but nothing was going to stop him now. Those magnificent gray-blue horns of Big Eye's with their fabulous double curl, like cloud wreaths above the patriarch's forehead, would literally be horns of plenty to the Marshall's. Once Fraser's money was theirs Karen would forget this "good neighbor" foolishness and admit he was right.

The mountain dawn grew spectrally, as Marshall climbed through a boulder-studded fairyland, majestic beyond reach of words. The high-country winter had taught him much. He had never really known these mountains until they had shown him their secret side, their winter face. But he knew them now. He had learned them in the cold and silence of long snow treks, from the peaks he had climbed, the frozen clothes and the dangers he had known on icy trails. Now the sharp colorless winter sunlight and the remote pine horizons piped him on and on—like the lure of gold at his diggings.

Today there was no sun, the sky was leaden from horizon to horizon. Marshall's trained eye raked the heights above for signs of sheep. They would be astir now, he knew, on the high ledges where they spent the night, pawing the snow away from the sparse dried grasses and lichens upon which they fed in winter. His chance of creeping up and surprising them was almost nil, for the vision of mountain sheep was telescopic, and Big Eye would surely be watching the lower slopes up which an enemy might climb. However, the breeze was with him, sucking downward from the peaks at this early hour, and there was a chance the sheep might emerge abruptly round some rocky outcrop within shooting range as they had numerous times in the past. In that case he would bag Big Eye first off and have the thing over with. He had never felt quite such a precipitate urge to get anything "over with," he realized uncomfortably.

Descendant of two generations of wilderness trail breakers, Marshall was a hunter born and had a sixth sense. He could sense danger, for instance, like an animal: on the breeze, on his skin, and in his shoulder blades and the tips of his hair. He was feeling something in all these ways this morning. Something not quite right with the air or with the mountain, he felt, but then, he usually felt like this after a dispute with Karen. At any rate, he was keeping an extra sharp lookout as he went.

Within an hour the slopes were giving way to the high-flung piles and parapets of Firetop's summit and still he had caught no glimpse of the sheep. No doubt he had been sighted long since from the lower slopes. He climbed slowly and warily. A wind rose toward midmorning, trailing snow out in wild white banners from the heights. It was a warm wind, a chinook, that came puffing through the passes to the southwest, bringing one of those mysterious lapses in the heart of winter, like a bit of May set down in February. Gradually it softened and sugared the surface of the snow till mountain and forest seemed to breathe again, though the true spring was weeks away.

Always these midwinter chinooks were fraught with peril in the mountains, for with the softening of the snow came the threat of avalanche.

Nat Marshall knew all about the menace of chinooks. He had been thinking about it in general and in particular as he climbed, for those sharp indefinable warnings had persisted. This was a time in which no sensible man would be climbing Firetop if he could possibly avoid it. It was unnerving even to Nat, who knew the mountain well. But toward midday he came to a ledge where the wild sheep had bunched together less than an hour before and the sight of that drove away all thought of danger.

The fresh trail wound upward along a series of narrow precipitous ledges, proof that Big Eye was alarmed. Most of the ledges overhung sheer drops of hundreds of feet and Marshall crept upward with catlike care. He had hoped to maneuver above the sheep and wait for a telling shot, but now, he knew, that was hopeless. He would have to be wily, indeed, to even come within gunshot, for he was a fair hunter and never resorted to tricks.

Among the upper rims he came upon a veritable wild-sheep city of winding streets and avenues where the snow had been tramped hard all winter by the hoofs of the flock. The huge tracks of Big Eye stood out, more than twice the size of any of the others, and Marshall knew that the boss ram was even bigger than he had suspected.

The going became softer, slipperier and more precarious, and a pair of eagles sailed close above Marshall as if waiting for some mischance to strike him down. It was a straight test of daring and agility now and Marshall felt out each foothold of the way, clinging by many a handhold as he went—only to discover that the sheep had quit the pinnacle by a secret way and made for another higher peak a mile beyond. Their fresh trail led down across a long saddle through deep snow and then upward again to the farther peak. Marshall followed. The trail became like a trench where the band had sunk belly-deep and bucked their way through the heavy drifts.

Marshall knelt and tightened the thongs of his snow-shoes, his blood beginning to race. Deep snow was a break in his favor. In such going he could outtravel the sheep with ease. He followed swiftly, moving on the surface of the snow to one side of the trail. Far below, on either side, the slopes of the saddle were darky furred with spruce and lodgepole. Even up here on the divide it was quite warm now, and roundabout could be heard the soft sucking chug of snowbanks collapsing under the thaw. Marshall quickened his stride, eager to be done with his mission and get out of this steep and dangerous area.

He had reached the halfway point of the saddle and had just sighted the sheep, moving dots on the far peak, when the grim thing happened. There was a whisper in the air. Marshall wondered for a moment if he were experiencing a touch of vertigo, so quietly and imperceptibly did the slide begin. It was as if the whole mountain were moving, so vast was the snow field. Another moment and the movement had become a rush.

With a yell Marshall flung himself back full length on the snow, holding his rifle aloft. The puny effort was quite ineffectual. Helpless, he went hurtling downward toward the line of dark evergreens far below, amidst a sound of rising thunder that echoed among the peaks. Momentarily his buried limbs were jerked and twisted from below as in a powerful rip tide, for the slide was like a living fluid thing churning in and sidewise upon itself. The power of it mounted as it rushed; in its wake it flung on high a wild white mane of foamlike snow.

The first ranks of the evergreens in its path were snapped off and swallowed up in its mighty maw. Momentarily splintered tree trunks were upended and tossed aloft like jackstraws, crossing, interlocking. From underneath the mass came hollow reports as boulders were wrenched from their moorings and clapped together.

Two minutes from its start the avalanche came to a stop, inert, silent, leaving in its wake a dirty gray swath scoured out of the face of the mountain. The great mass of the slide quite filled the cup of the pine-clad valley four thousand feet below its starting point. Upon the breast of the slide lay a jumble of broken branches, bark, earth and splinters of wood and rock. In the midst of it all, like a bit of debris half buried in snow, lay Nat Marshall.

Another hour and a half passed and the jagged peaks roundabout leaned toward night, before the man stirred and raised himself with a groan. A break had come in the chinook and the wind was veering to the east. It was the bite of growing cold that had roused Marshall from the stupor in which he had lain since something had struck him a blow on the head.

At his first movement sharp pain stabbed his memory awake. He recalled then the blow and his pitching downward into darkness—a darkness which he had thought was the end. For a space now he lay back taking stock of his predicament. Beside him was his rifle which he had miraculously maintained through all that frantic ride, and his hunter's nerve was restored by the touch. Carefully he moved his limbs. One knee was badly wrenched and a hot pain shot up his side when he moved it, but no bones were broken. Except for his throbbing head and groggy senses he was unhurt. But his snowshoes were gone, torn from his feet by the churning mass of the slide, lost beyond finding. And without them he was like a cripple on the icy mountain. All around him now Marshall heard faint snicking sounds as the half-melted snow on the mountainside hardened into ice at its moorings. Snow was beginning to fall again, not the soft fluff of the night before but stinging hard pellets that warned of storm. A February blizzard was a terrible thing on the roof of the world and the wind keened of it in the branches of the few trees left standing. The truth came home to Marshall like a knife thrust. He was a good ten miles from home, lame, and without snowshoes, with wild mountain country stretching in between. He must have a good shelter for the night in order to survive, for already the cold was eating up his small reserve of strength.

His rifle trailing in one hand he began to climb doggedly upgrade, part of the time crawling on all fours. It was a weak effort, and his progress was tortuously slow. He had no idea where shelter could be found, but he would not meet the night and the storm lying down.

It was as he was rounding the bulk of a great fallen tree that blocked his path that the abrupt and unbelievable thing occurred. The snow suddenly gave way beneath him and with a muffled yell Marshall slid head foremost into a yawning hole that had opened up beneath the roots. He brought up in darkness some six feet below, still clutching his rifle, his knee throbbing from the strain it had received, but pleasantly aware all at once of sudden warmth, of quiet and a surcease from the biting mountain wind. This cranny or recess into which he had fallen, it appeared, was the very sanctuary for which he had prayed. He put out a hand to feel about him in the dimness—and in that moment knew real terror.

His hand had contacted a shaggy breathing form in the darkness and simultaneously he became cognizant of what his woods-wise nose had been trying to telegraph to his brain for some moments. An odor filled his nostrils, the warm pungent odor of carnivore. Instinct told him the creature beside him was a sleeping bear.

Marshall's heart was hammering, his blood racing hot and cold. The only bear in the Firetop region so far as he knew was Old Gray, the silvertip grizzly, that savage killer of sheep and cattle which had long been the terror of the heights. His hand flew to his rifle, for all grizzlies were mankillers. Then his exploring fingers found four matches in one of his pockets. He risked one of the precious sticks as well as the chance of swift annihilation for a look at the sleeping beast.

It was Old Gray beyond a doubt. The monster lay relaxed and peaceful, sunk in the heavy torpor of the hibernation sleep. The air of the cave was filled with the low, slow sound of his breathing and was tempered by the warmth radiating from the huge body. Nat Marshall marveled at the size of the brute. The gray-brown bulk loomed boulder-large, the great head almost as wide as Marshall's body. The animal must weigh all of fifteen hundred pounds, he judged. He gazed fascinated until the match burned his fingers.

His first impulse was to put a bullet through the giant's brain as it slept and thus do away with all danger, but hard upon that sane logic began to function. In his ears was the keening of the wind, reminding him grimly of the world of death and cold outside and the miracle that had shuffled him into this place of shelter and protection. He might as easily have ended up beneath tons of snow or frozen as he lay unconscious in the cutting wind. Here was the only haven on all Firetop in which to weather such a storm. The very warmth of his enemy would keep him alive.

But why class Old Gray as enemy? The grizzly had never actually harmed him. He was, as Karen had said, a neighbor on the mountain. In his weakened state the concept took on mystical meaning to Marshall. His panic urge to destroy was fear-born, part of the killer that made up the hunter, the thing Karen always fought. His thoughts flew to her now and what she must be going through and he strove to send her reassurance. Always there had been a sort of telepathic field between them when separated. Often Marshall had explained to her the various mishaps that may befall a hunter and the many things an experienced woodsman can do to offset storm and catastrophe. He wove his thoughts with strength and faith and presently knew a peace that he felt must have its source in the home cabin.

In the back of Marshall's mind was a dread that the man smell permeating the den would impress the torpid senses of the grizzly and rouse him to attack. For two hours, while the night deepened and the storm grew, he lay close to the heaving fur-clad form in a sweat of anxiety, scarcely daring to move. Now and then he would stiffen throughout, as the monster stirred in its sleep and twin blasts of breath whistled through its nostrils. But gradually he became too weary even for trepidation. A very drunkenness of exhaustion and reaction was upon him. His senses flagged and he slept.

For twenty-four hours thereafter Marshall did nothing but rest and sleep and think, while outside the storm blew itself out. Throughout that time the warmth radiating from his huge bedfellow was the one thing that kept him functioning. Old Gray was a cozy base-burner; one, moreover, which needed no fuel or watching. The vast organic warmth of him tempered the den and kept the air hole automatically open at the top despite the drifting snow, which almost covered it at times. Marshall's gratitude to the sleeping beast became bottomless.

Noon of the second day brought a direct light through the cave opening above, strong enough for Marshall to note casually, and with weird detachment, the grim mien of the grizzly, the savagery of the porcine, slightly upturned muzzle, the folds like worry wrinkles in the broad receding forehead that was streaked with gray. The grizzly's stomach was flat and empty, for that was the way bears went into winter sleep, and so there was surprisingly little of the rank carnivore scent in the cave. The walls of the den were formed of earth and rock strengthened by the interlaced roots of an overturned pine.

Marshall's fear lest the grizzly awake had gradually relaxed; the sluggishness of hibernation was too heavy upon Old Gray, he saw; a stupor akin to death itself. He sensed the hand of a watchful Providence in the far-flung chance that had led him to the grizzly's den in this bottom hour. It was that ninth part of the hair of chance that old hunters sometimes spoke of; a thing unthinkable, beyond belief. And what a tale it would make to relate round campfires in years to come!

It was during those long dark hours that Marshall knew that the original mishap of the snowslide had been no mere accident, that the wheel of things had definitely slipped into reverse for him. There is a grim hour, he had learned from years in the open, that comes in the life of every man, striking at a time when he is least expectant, least prepared; an hour of fate in which all that he had garnered for good or evil is balanced against him. Such a time was preceded by certain warnings, often too subtle to be read. Marshall was no mystic, but a hunter, yet he had sensed many promptings, and now he suddenly knew all about them. There had been many little indications of small import, yet enough had they been heeded. And there had been Karen.

Within him all former thoughts of the hunter and killer were melting away like snow before some chinook of the heart. For in the stress of those hours he had sloughed off for the time being all usual habit of thought, letting an inner knowledge that was nothing more or less than intuition reign instead. Not once did he think of Big Eye or Fraser or the promised reward.

In between his thinking and sleeping Marshall ate thankfully but sparingly of the package of food Karen had put in his Mackinaw pocket. There was enough to last for days if need be. For drink he ate handful after handful of the fresh-fallen snow.

Another morning and a blue-white filter of light came through the roof of the cave, telling of a bright clear sky in the world without. The wind had dropped. Marshall stood up and broke away a sizable hole into the open air. Through it he thrust his rifle, then slowly drew himself out of the den while its shaggy owner slept peacefully on with Marshall's blessing. The still cold that follows a storm cut into him as he stood up. The glare of sunlight upon the new snow stabbed his optic nerves, threatening him with the perilous snow blindness, but that would not deter him now.

His one problem was to get down the mountain alive. All thought of the wild sheep band had been formally banished from mind. His prolonged hunt for the head of Big Eye, he saw, had been a special thing, and not a good thing. Had he laid the old patriarch low he would have shattered one of the natural right things of Nature, a perfection beyond perfection. Karen had said that in her own way, but he had had to find it out in his. He wasn't good at words, but he would find a way to tell her about it and how his heart had been one for a space with the wild heart of the mountain and found a certain grace.

Up a long slanting course through the deep new snow he scrambled toward the westward-facing slopes that would drop him down to his cabin. It was only now as he climbed that he sensed in the deeper folds of being how very near the end he had been. Only because in his life as a hunter he had achieved some harmony with Nature and the wild creatures had he been given a bit of leeway, he saw. And with this came many realizations, things too often coated over throughout a man's entire life. They were not the sort of things that could be written down or put in words. Great inchoate truths, rather, that dwelt in the underconsciousness, dim realizations that had hovered near but had not been seized upon, felt rather than known. Outwardly he was his cool, sporting self again, but within, he knew, he would never be the same again.

Lost in his thinking he was utterly unprepared for what confronted him on the pinnacle above. Rounding a jutting rock on the heights, he came abruptly upon the bighorn band huddled on a ledge no more than a hundred feet ahead of him. They were clustered in the partial shelter of an outcrop of rock, and, by the look, they had been there a long time. Marshall stood stone-still, watching. Now that he had foresworn killing Big Eye he had apparently succeeded in surprising the band, a feat well-nigh impossible with so wily a quarry. But his moment of triumph was hollowed by the irony of the thing.

Came a dry snoofing challenge in the air and a ram pressed forward through a cluster of ewes and faced Marshall, shaking his head belligerently. Gripping his rifle, the man leaned against the rock wall, waiting in wonder, for there was something queer about the situation. The milling sheep made no move to flee. Was there another enemy on the ledge beyond the sheep which they feared more than they feared man? And where was Big Eye? The ram facing Marshall was another, younger beast. Had the old patriarch been injured or abnegated to a stronger ram?

The situation was an ugly one. The trail Marshall was on led along the sheep's ledge, the only trail leading across the rims. It looked as if the ram might attack, or at least contest his passing. If so, he would have to shoot straight and fast. A mountain sheep could carry a lot of lead. If his first shot did not kill, the ram might charge and, if so, he could make short work of a man on a narrow ledge with no chance to dodge.

Marshall advanced angrily half a dozen paces, weapon ready. For a moment the outcome hung at a teetery balance; then the sheep broke before him, falling back in a wave, the belligerent young ram moving last of all, head still toward Marshall and stamping in defiance.

Then the man saw Big Eye. He had not moved with the others, did not stir now. Legs doubled under him he was bedded down in a recess beneath ovehanging rock, gazing out over the backs of his followers across a gulf of valleys toward a far peak. Marshall paused again in wonder, while Big Eye's band continued to retreat, most of them moving backward, still eying their leader. The patriarch moved not a muscle; the swirling gusts of the heights lifted and stirred the fleece of his heavy coat, but he gave no sign.

Suddenly Marshall knew: The old ram would move no more. He had been winter-killed during the recent storm, meeting his end as the wisest and noblest of his kind so often did, bedded down among the high rims over which he ruled, victorious to the last against all the machinations of man. Out of loyalty and loss and a sense of protection, his band had stayed by their leader's side, even challenging their greatest enemy.

Marshall climbed up and stood before the fallen one with something like reverence. The big stone-gray eyes of the ram with their Oriental capsule-shaped pupils were wide and set in death—the head still proudly and unflinchingly lifted, like a figure in noble stone. Those glorious crinkled horns, with their coveted flare and double curl, clasped the monarch's head like twin cornucopias of fable. . . . Horns of plenty and promise, his now for the taking, Marshall thought, and it was in his mind that he would come back and take that head next day. But deep-down, he knew he would not. In death more than ever the old ram and the mountain were one. He still belonged to his people, to the cold and the snow and the rare and secret heights.

▪ Trumpeter of the Air Lanes

IT WAS A LAND OF ONE UNENDING HORIZON. AS FAR AS THE
eye could reach, on every side, stretched the limitless reaches
of the muskeg—low, flat and newborn land, an amphibious
blend of swamp and sandbar and steely reach of sea. A treeless land, it lay far up near the roof of the world, beyond the
limit of even the juniper and the dwarf spruce, where the
upper section of the great Barren Grounds begins to stretch
out an arm through unbroken desolation across the Northwest Passage to the Pole.

Here, beyond the frontiers of man's unknown, in the endless reed-grown sphagnum swamps that fringe the Arctic
Sea, was the one domain where human footprints and handi-
work had never touched—the last stronghold of the kingdom
of birds. A hunter's paradise which no hunter had yet seen,
save perhaps the little Innuits, or the wandering Eskimos.

Summer had just come to the muskeg. Between darkness
and daylight it came, routing all in a night the last forces of
winter—for there is no spring in the Far North. Last night
had been dark and ominous with cutting gusts of wind,
filled with the threat of sleet and ice; today, from the south
and east as the mists began to lift, warm zephyrs came puf-

17

fing with a melting, ineffable tenderness, as if earth, air and sun had met in a long swooning embrace.

Now it was that the countless squadrons of wild birds began to arrive from the Southland. The few flocks of early migrants who had been lingering for days about the icy tidewaters, uttering faint, disappointed cries, flew screaming here and there as they chose their nesting places. All that day the flocks beat up from the south, filling the sky until all the waterways to the horizon and beyond were filled with birds, nothing but birds. The babel of their myriad voices ran in a watery murmur over the land, filling earth and sky, as they flew and swam, floated, dived, quarreled, fed and courted, in that abandon that comes only where man is never known to stalk.

Toward the end of that day a great hullabaloo swept the miles of feeding flocks over the arrival of the real royalty of the air—four great troops of swans and golden cranes, who migrate as a rule at the same time and fly at the same cloudy height. From high sky the first far, infinitesimal cry of the swans came wafting to earth just as the horizontal rays of the setting sun began to turn from orange to crimson. Their calls came ringing like the faint treble notes of huntsmen's horns, sounded miles and miles away, with now and then a deeper note as of a military trumpet from the giant leaders, as the swan flock tipped majestically earthward, winding down from the clouds as if along some invisible spiral stairway.

In all nature there is no sound more stirring to man, bird or animal, than the trumpeter swan's call, that wild, unearthly trumpet note that comes floating down from the clouds in early spring and fall.

Their graceful descent into the waters of the little lake was a sight of beauty, awesome as the flight of angels, their

vast wings flashing snow-white against the blue enamel of
the sky while the sunset struck ruby glow from their flawless
breasts. Not for an instant did they break their strict wedge-
shaped flight formation. As if in homage to the coming of
these kings, every flock of birds for miles around sprang
suddenly upward in unison as at a prearranged signal.

The swan flock, unmoved, came to anchor in the lake with
many tremendous splashings and loud bugling calls and horn
notes expressing infinite peace and satisfaction. For a time
they swam here and there over the still water, preening their
plumage and stretching their long necks after their almost
nonstop flight from the blue and gold lagoons of faraway
Mexico. They rode high and proudly on the water like great
white liners among a lot of dingy colliers.

There were twenty-seven birds in the white flock that
had led the northern flight—not the familiar whistlers, but
those long-distance kings of the air lanes known as trumpeter
swans, the largest and stateliest birds of which the American
continent can boast. Each bird had a wing spread of over
eight feet, while the great clarion-throated leaders exceeded
even that. The pure white of their plumage, radiant and
flawless, was balanced and set off with artistic effect by the
polished jet black of their bills and legs. Noncombative by
nature, only by their great size and an aloof majesty was
their kingship among the flocks maintained, though when
pressed they were capable of a fierce offensive which even
the sea eagle and the fierce gyrfalcon had learned to avoid.

Scattered here and there over the muskeg were the remains of broken watchtowers of mud and sticks—all that the
winter storms had left of the last year's nests of the swans.
They stood out boldly along the waterways, in full view of
every marauder of the waste, for the trumpeter swan, like
the bald eagle, scorns to hide its nest, and fears no foe of

earth or air. The great leader of the flock and his chosen
mate swam at once to their old familiar nesting place, on a
narrow spit of land that jutted into the lake. Here on the
outermost point they had built their nest for nine consecu-
tive years, for the swan, like sensible men and all the more
highly evolved animals, takes one mate for life.

Little was left of their last year's home but the mud foun-
dation, but both birds set diligently to work rebuilding, the
male working with the same zeal as his mate—collecting
dead sticks, moss and brushwood from all around the lake
shore where the winds and floods had driven them.

On the very day the leader's nest was completed his mate
began to lay, lining the cup of the nest with down as she
went on sitting. When she was through there were four vast
eggs in the nest, full five inches long and a dozen in circum-
ference, colored a dull buff gray. Throughout the long and
arduous labor of sitting the male swan, unfailing in devotion
and the court etiquette of his royal caste, remained constantly on guard near the nest and became the bringer of
food.

At last, five weeks and two days from the laying of the
first egg, came a morning when the patient brooding mother
heard faint stirrings and tappings, and infinitesimal cries
rising from the four warm eggs beneath her breast. From
time to time she would lower her head among them to listen
with a rapture unequaled by any other mother among birds.
Her mate drew close to the nest, wings spread and flapping,
but never relaxing his fierce watchfulness for the enemies
that never came.

Two hours later the first young cygnet, after long and
ordered rapping, split the top off his confining shell, and,
thrusting it aside like the lid of a box, struggled forth all
damp, bare and blind against his mother's breast. Within the

next hour two other eggs hatched in the same manner, and the mother swan was half standing in the nest to give the naked sprawlers room. Furious excitement swept both parent birds all that day. They forgot to feed, and the old male marched up and down, flapping his wings at intervals and stretching himself to his full height to sound a loud and sonorous trumpet call.

The process of weaning was hurried forward apace by the anxious parent birds, for the Arctic summer is frighteningly short; it waits on no frailties, and the young cygnets had much to gain in strength and wisdom before entering upon the rigors of the long southern flight that fall.

One morning in the third week the mother swan without warning tipped them all gently but firmly over the edge of the nest, where they fell squawking on the damp ground beneath. Then they had their first trip by water. Of course they could swim from the first moment, and it was only second nature for them to imitate their parents by tipping up and thrusting their long necks under water after tempting roots. The next few days were one ceaseless foraging expedition as the family swam up and down the waterways in search of food.

These were days filled with danger for the young ones. The parent birds, as has been said, feared no enemy but man, but they could not keep all the brood constantly under their eyes. Each day fierce hunting goshawks swooped low over the little family, waiting a chance when one of the youngsters should stray, to pounce and deliver the fatal stroke of their kind.

For a month danger was held at a distance by the watchful parents. Then came the first lessons in flying. Owing to their increasing bulk, racing and winning against their growing strength, the brood rebelled, as is the usual thing, long after

their stiff flight feathers had grown, at the ordeal of master-
ing the higher life of the air. But one morning the parents
forced the issue in a clever manner they had learned by
chance. Both the old birds, calling insistently to the youngsters to follow, set off in a low skimming flight across a
stretch of quaking bog. The brood followed along the
ground until they sank belly deep in the swamp mud. Instinctively then each youngster beat the air desperately with
his well-feathered wings until—miracle of miracles—all found
themselves wavering upward in their first trial flight. That
is, all but the weakest of the four, the timid one of the family. For some reason the development of this little one had
been retarded, so that she was no more than two-thirds the
size of her companions. The instant she sank in the viscous
mud, terror gripped her and she lay flat, calling pitifully as
she sank, until even her wings became mired and flight was
impossible! The parent birds did not notice that one of the
brood had been left behind until from mid-sky the male
swan caught sight of a flashing golden meteor that fell hissing earthward—a great sea eagle, whose prism-binocular eyes
had noted the little drama in the bog from a mile high and
turned it quickly into tragedy.

Long before the parents could wing back to the rescue the
lone emperor of the northern skyways was flapping upward, bearing a still, limp form in his talons. The swans gave
hopeless chase, but dared not go far and leave the remainder
of their brood unprotected.

A week later disaster struck another blow at the family.
Having conquered fear in their first flight, the youngsters
now went to the other extreme—the fever to show off. Like
many a novice in aeronautics they already hankered for
stunt flying. They spent hours each day flapping into the
eye of the wind, then volplaning back in great looping arcs

to where their parents fed, gabbling and trumpeting with excitement.

It was a gusty day, and the swan brood were at their wind-riding, while the old birds watched. The swiftest of the three persisted in flapping higher and farther than the others in spite of whistled warnings. Caught aloft in a sudden fierce updraft, he was unable to make a landing and was swept many hundred yards down the wind plump into the company of cruel and thieving skuas, fierce, dark, hawklike birds, who among other things are cannibals. A high insensate yelping from a hundred pirate throats told the parent birds the culmination of the youngster's rashness.

With a deep trumpeting challenge, the male swan rose in the air and hurtled down the wind like a projectile, straight into the gray cloud of the meat birds, sprung suddenly from heaven knows where, eddying and screaming in a dark maelstrom about a flapping tearing tangle on the ground. The center of that tangle was the luckless little swan.

Not until two of their number lay dead, shaken to death in the skua's steel-like mandibles, and two others went staggering away dragging broken wings, did the killers withdraw, and then it was only to take up the crueler game of waiting.

The battle was theirs at all events, and well they knew it. All settled on the mud at a safe distance, and folding their wings about them like old men wrapped in heavy overcoats, they huddled in dense ranks and proceeded to demonstrate the horrible patience the sea had taught them through the ages. Whatever happened, a banquet of meat would presently be laid for them there.

The cold moon that night looked down on one of those pitiable situations of bird life. All through the night the father swan stayed on guard over his helpless little one, pac-

ing up and down and answering now and then the anxious
call of his mate by the lake shore hundreds of yards away.
There was nothing to be done but watch, while the flutter-
ing of the wounded one grew weaker and finally stilled, but
not until twenty-four hours more had passed did the big
male cease his grim and hopeless vigil.

The thin, bittersweet melancholy of the Arctic summer
drew to a close. There came another day of swift change. A
phalanx of dun-gray clouds that seemed to have been waiting just beyond the horizon spread over the upper sky, turning the gold of the sunlight to a dim sulphur hue. All in a
few hours the brooding desolation of autumn had spread
over the land.

In a few days flocks of smaller, frailer flyers like the
thrushes and martins began to decamp. Of all the clans the
swans alone showed little excitement, though the seasoned
leaders constantly looked to the north and watched the shift-
ing wind. By the time the sun had gone behind the permanent slate-black clouds of winter for that year but a half
dozen of the larger clans remained. Among these were the
green-backed teal, the hardy brants and Canada geese, and
the cranes, all of which had learned to wait on the subtler
wisdom of the swans for final storm warnings.

The last of September had come, and the pond margins
were musical with the tinkle of shell ice before the first of
these departed. It was the next day in the first driving flakes
of a coming storm that the swan leaders sounded a hoarse,
sonorous rally call and a minute later beat majestically into
the wind, funneling upward in a series of great circles, followed closely by the cranes.

Slowly they rose to the giddy height of nearly three miles
before they straightened out, and, with considerable jealous
bickering among the younger birds for position, formed

themselves into three baseless triangles of misty white and swept down the sky on the wings of the gale.

Over the empty expanses of the Barrens they passed in the first two days, stopping only at night to feed nervously in some still remote lake. Then beneath them the green-black forested lands of trappers and hunters began to unroll—the beginning of that vast territory ruled by the Hudson's Bay Company, where every furred and feathered thing runs a constant gauntlet of death. Here nine members of the white squadron fell to guns of trained sharpshooters, among them the female of the two remaining young ones of the leader's brood.

She was flying close to her brother toward the end of the long wedge, when the high whine of the bullets cut among them. A dull thud, an explosion of feathers filling the air like a white geyser, and the young female was suddenly gone from the ranks. For a minute her brother saw her beating desperately along, fifty yards below him, straining to keep up, then her struggle ceased and on her wings she pitched earthward, while up through the rare air came a high plaintive whistling note, like the soft running of an octave, fainter and fainter till it faded to a mere filament of an echo and was gone.

It was the first time the young male had heard the death song of his kind, that sad, unearthly cadence that in coming years was to ring continually in his ears. For a moment his wild black eyes held a stricken look, and he dropped suddenly from the ranks as if to hurtle downward in the path of the playmate with whom he had become inseparable. Other young ones also fell out, but only for a moment or two were the ranks demoralized. The old leader slowed the flight as if to circle back, and with a hoarse bugling call brought order out of the panic; the line closed up; then the flight swept ruthlessly onward and upward beyond the range of rifles.

These casualties were graver to their dwindling numbers than any human could reckon. For the remaining two thousand miles of their journey they would be beset with constant danger. In all America there was no spot where their hunted clan could be free of the far-reaching tentacles of the feather-trade octopus.

In the next two days the trumpeters overtook many of the smaller flyers who had left the Arctic weeks before and tarried in the northern states.

In Texas and Oklahoma many of the clanging hosts of geese and ducks dropped out; Florida claimed the bulk of the remaining flocks, but the swans and cranes had learned long since to be decoyed by nothing on American soil. Ahead of them was another seven-hundred-mile carry to the unsettled forests of Mexico.

Two days more and the flock sighted once more the rank green solitudes of the jungles where lay the chain of palm-fringed lagoons that were their winter haven. Many other birds were there before them; from aloft the flock caught the flash of white wings open and waving on the water below, signal of welcome and safety. In the depths of the tangled jungle that was like a still, vast hothouse the flock took up their winter quarters.

During long, changeless days in which there was never any cold or wind, the one remaining princeling of the flock, the only son of the old leader, slowly changed his first travel coat of rusty gray for one of flawless white.

His powerful sinuous neck took on a high, proud arch; he gazed long, as all swans do, at his image in the water; and spent hours each day preening the snow of his plummage with deft touches of his bill, as a woman dresses her hair.

That spring hunters were thicker along the flyways than ever before. It was in this migration, as the flock dipped one night over a Missouri marsh, that a red flash leaped out of the dark with a thunderous roar, and the young prince's mother collapsed from her place near the head of the ranks. Flight slowed, the old leader made as if to circle back, but, seeing his mate lying still on the surface of the water, he swept the ranks resolutely on again. But thereafter something was gone from the soul and efficiency of the flock.

Weeks later, in the Arctic, the old king sought his familiar nesting place once more, but he took no mate, and his lonely cry was ever echoing over the waters as he searched the skyways for a flashing white form he knew. He associated with none but his son, for the swan breaks all rules of bird gregariousness.

It was not until the following spring that the young prince brought back with him a mate from the Southland, a beautiful, flawless young creature with whom he had often swum, fed and flown. Theirs was one of the few new nests reared on the muskeg that year, for during the last two flights the flock had been cut down by fully half. Their relation was full of devotion and an unfailing and gallant attention. That year their nest contained no eggs, and it was well for them, for it was the most perilous year the flock had known.

Again hunters were waiting along every travel way, and it was in the height of his first love year that the young prince's mate fell to the boom of four-gauge shotguns as the flock crossed the Mississippi from Tennessee. The young male saw her flapping frantically below him in a vain struggle to keep aloft, then she pitched toward the water in a wobbling arc. For a moment he broke rank, uttering loud treble calls, then a sharp bass note from his sire swept him on again.

But that night the young prince broke every precedent of the flight laws of his kind. It was as if the very driving force of his life and instincts had been left behind him, and the evening saw him returning, a glinting rose-white speck in the last of the sunset, as he circled calling above the broad river waters.

It happened that the hunters who had lain in wait that day were out after live birds and had aimed to wing their quarry. They had captured two other birds, but by some miracle the young female had eluded them in the dense undergrowth alongshore, though they searched until dark. So it was that her mate found her that night, where she had hidden herself deep among the rushes.

Before morning both had stolen away from the danger zone. The female could no longer fly. Her right wing was broken and her white breast plowed by the heavy shot, but her swimming was still unimpaired. For four days and four nights the pair kept to the broad river course, swimming downstream. Time and again they were sighted by men or dogs, and hunters turned out with clubs and guns, but the death cordons never quite closed upon them.

They took refuge at last in the swampy bayous of Louisiana, but it was two weeks more before the female could rise from the water in a short, feeble flight. Then followed weeks of tortuous passage down the Gulf of Mexico, the pair half starved and buffeted by rain and wind, keeping to the only safety they knew, beyond the shoreward breakers. Only at dead of night did they venture to land to feed hurriedly in the harsh salt marshes.

But each day the female could wing a bit longer and farther, and by December they had won the last tortuous lap of the seven-hundred-mile carry down the treacherous waters of the Gulf to their old familiar sanctuary among the Mexican lagoons.

The old king of the flock was not there to meet them. He, with scores of others, had failed to win through the gauntlet of high-powered rifles that year, and had gone to meet his long-mourned mate. When the flight time came again in April, hunters marked that less than a hundred trumpeters all told came through on the northern flight.

Two years later at the great Hudson's Bay Company's post at Ile-a la Crosse, headquarters of the vast feather traffic of all the north country, Neil McDonald, the factor of the post, sat in his office on a day in November going over his books. For fifteen years it had been his particular duty to keep a written record of the rapid sinking of the feather-trade barometer for the great company which dealt in death.

Fifty years ago no entry showed less than 1,300 swans taken per annum, but the past two decades showed a rapid decline, the figures dropping to less than fifty birds for a run of years. Then abruptly they sank like the tail of a fever chart till the final two years' entries showed but nine and three respectively. And this year saw the end, the zero mark.

At the bottom of the page opposite the year, McDonald had written in his crabbed hand, "No entry." Beneath it he presently drew two broad black lines, then closed the ledger upon a graphic story in black and white facts, of the passing of the most stately and beautiful of all birds from American soil.

That year word went forth that the trumpeter swans were no longer coming through. Learned men from the colleges were led to write belated papers on the subject, for from Mexico to Canada hunters had sighted no single trumpeter flock that fall.

But men were wrong in their surmises; the trumpeters were not all gone. Today, if you look for them wisely and long enough, you will still find a small flock making the long traverse each year, but they no longer follow the beaten air lanes of birds. They have been driven westward. Like the tern, the cranes, and a few others of the wisest and most hunted of the flocks, they have learned in time to take the perilous water route, which none but the high-powered kings of the air may follow. Straight down the wind-swept Pacific from British Columbia they travel, to lower California, and thence across the unsettled parts of Mexico— 2,600 miles, to their old goal among the sequestered tropic lagoons. There are never more than twenty of them, they travel high and out of sight of land, and they are wise in the ways of men and guns. Always they must battle for days against the heavy sea winds, they grow lean from lack of feeding along the route, but they know that neither hunger nor the elements can be half so cruel as man. For their wary old leader, once the princeling of the old-time flock, has taught them all he learned since the long-ago day when he first defied flock law and learned a new resourcefulness, for the sake of his wounded mate.

▪ Search for the Fire Bird

SINCE EARLY MORNING MAYHEW HAD BEEN THREADING THE mazes of the river bush, following faint animal paths, his shotgun held in both hands ready for instant use. His gaze as always was upon the treetops, forever seeking a flash of the flame-colored feathers that might signal the end of his quest. It was perhaps the fiftieth day of just such tactics and one of the hardest of them all, yet his eagerness and expectancy was in no wise lulled. Fifty days of watching and stalking, surrounded by hardly believable privations and dangers, spied upon by inimical eyes he felt but rarely saw.

For fifteen years Mayhew had girdled the globe in his strange quest for rare birds. He had given the world six fabulous collections of avian life, including the black swan of the far south, the ethereal sylph, the quetzal of Mexico and Central America, the manakin, the umbrella bird and the almost mystical Alaskan murrelet and its equally mythical eggs. All were species never before shown in the western world. Just now he was out after specimens of the fabulous cock-of-the-rock, known as Flame of the Forest, said to inhabit this portion of the Colombian jungles.

In almost two months Mayhew had been unable to sight a

single specimen of the flame bird. The natives along the
river were maddeningly noncommittal when it came to actual directions. Time and again he had seen the quetzal and
the black umbrella bird. The latter was a name to conjure
with. The natives called them "crows" and often shot them,
they said. Mayhew had caught four specimens, almost worth
his trip alone. But the flame-red cock-of-the-rock, for which
he sought, continued to baffle him utterly. The closest he had
gotten to the trail of his quarry had been a myth from the
mouth of an undersized native hunter in a nearby village,
that the "Fire Bird" lived back yonder, pointing in the
general direction of the mountains, and that he had shot two
not long ago to make a stew. A stew—this bird so rare that
no museum in the world yet possessed a specimen, and no
zoo, though tropical expeditions had long kept a sharp eye
out for a glimpse of him and his nesting place.

Lately Mayhew had begun to imagine that there was
something of the malignancy of this land in his frustration.
He did not fear Colombia—the choking jungles he had
crawled through where sunlight never touched the earth,
the perennial rains, fevers and miasmas and suffocating heat.
He had become peculiarily immune, for a white man, to all
these things. But he had to admit that the jungle had out-
played him. If the cock-of-the-rock really dwelt in this
region—then Colombia guarded it well.

Its forests teemed with myriads of birds of every hue, and
gorgeous butterflies that rivaled its orchids in brilliance, and
scores of different hummingbirds and a dozen species of
monkeys whose bent was to jeer and mock the explorer on
his way. Mayhew relived the two occasions on which he
had thought for a few minutes his quest was ended. Once it
had been the flight of a band of red and green parrots over
the jungle roof; the second time it was a cock quetzal plum-

ing himself in a high tree, with the sun glinting on his carmine vest. . . . All to do over again.

"The cock-of-the-rock doesn't nest here, that's all," he had begun to tell himself repeatedly the past few days. "It simply doesn't live anywhere, outside the ornithology books."

It had rained intermittently since dawn—half-hour downpours followed by periods of partial sunlight and mist, in a steam-bath atmosphere that seemed to suck out through the pores the very elements that made one human. There had not been a day but what it had rained thus. In the humidity the trees became mere supports for moss and fungus which grew on and over the whole world, strangling life; piling layer upon layer on rocks and rotting stumps, hanging from the branches, swathing all the tree trunks. During the downpours Mayhew would take out his oilskin raincoat and wait beneath one of the great trees that seemed coeval with the dawn of creation. When the rain ceased he would move on again through the ceaseless drip of the broad leaves.

All morning he had been following one of the nameless little tributaries of the Fragua River. About midafternoon the trail he followed dipped down into a jungle of eight-foot grass where the footing was spongy, and water seeped up in the tracks he left. He would be out of the grass in a few minutes, he thought, and pressed on; but somewhat later, reaching a rise of ground, he saw that the grass jungle stretched away limitlessly to all sides, a great savanna of secret waterways that skirted the base of a mountain rising abruptly from the jungle floor.

It was as he stood there that he heard numerous dry clacking sounds not far away that he took to be the cries of bittern. And then he began to smell something bad in the still, hot air. It was a thick, sweet, horrible smell that caught at the nose like musk. A peculiar uneasiness began stealing over him. Subconsciously he had an idea what that smell was, though his conscious mind did not accept the fact till a terrifying snarling bellow echoed over the savanna. The still air quivered with the immense cavernous vibration. Other snarlings answered it. Saurians, of course; big bull 'gators that doubtless plied up and down these waterways from the distant river.

Mayhew had decided to turn back along the soggy way he had come, when he detected movement here and there in the long grass along his back trail. This maze of pathways was evidently a saurian city. The creatures had scented him and were converging along his trail, a bloodlust fomenting in their low reptilian skulls. And he armed with nothing but a shotgun designed for birds.

Still he was not particularly perturbed. Mayhew knew alligators after a fashion, but he had never known them on the loose in their natural breeding grounds, in a region where men did not hunt them. What he saw, therefore, a minute later, did not look true. It could not be true—the monster that went slithering across one of the waterways below him—a creature twenty feet or more in length. Its bulk seemed to drag endlessly across the grass-bordered trail, from immense gaping mouth to the ridged and armored tail, all of it of a dull mud color, as if part of the earth had got up and moved.

Purpose evaporated from Mayhew's mind. Not for anything now would he have ventured back the way he had come. He struck out for the high ground at the base of the distant mountain, some three thousand yards away. It would take him far out of his way in his return to his base at the Indian village downriver, but anything was preferable to remaining longer in this domain of dragons.

He came to a soggy depression where water oozed up to his ankles. Off to his right was a miniature lake or pond with rush-grown banks. Abruptly a great patch of muddy earth before him came to life, rose and hurtled toward the lake. Two big alligators rushed to the water's edge and plunged in, sinking from sight in the stagnant depths, obeying an inborn instinct to flee to water when surprised. Mayhew had looked right at the brutes without seeing them, so well camouflaged were their mud-caked bodies.

A sweat began to stand out on Mayhew's face as he picked his way along an overarched trail. Rustlings and various slithering sounds from the rear told him that 'gators were gathering along his trail. What breeze there was, he noted, was in his face. The creatures apparently tracked by scent. And once they had scented prey, they were not man-shy.

Mayhew's blood suddenly raced hot and cold again. Directly across his path something gleaming and grayish looped like a spout of water. A fifteen-foot grass boa went slithering from sight into the rushes, quite possibly as intent on escape from what was coming as he himself.

As he hurried on along winding, oozy ways, Mayhew experienced fears such as must have haunted prehistoric man in his war against the monsters that beset him. For this sunken place of grass and waterways was out of all time, a region left over from remote ages, unchanged by man, where the great reptiles still were kings. Not far behind him he knew that the saurians followed inexorably along his trail, sluggishly, ponderously, but doubtless with gathering momentum now. The horrible part was the tremendous gulf that lay between. It was not like being stalked by warm-blooded beasts. There was no quelling such creatures with the eye; no quality of their natures a man could touch or play upon.

Mayhew's nerves were taut from strain and the fierce urge at the seat of his plexus to run headlong toward the high ground; yet a fear of what might lurk along the trail ahead made him repress the impulse. But he hurried, as fast as prudence allowed, trying to keep to the most open trails.

But by the time he sighted the base of the mountain ahead his heart sank again. For what he saw was an almost perpendicular rampart of rock and earth rising directly from the savanna floor and stretching away as far as he could see. The cliff had been cut out by the little stream he had followed all morning. He could not have approached the mountain at a more inaccessible spot. From the outset, Colombia itself had seemed arrayed against him like a shadowy third.

The mountain was his way of escape. No time now to follow along its base, searching an easier way up; the afternoon light was already waning. Mayhew chose a spot beneath a small tree which grew out of the face of the embankment forty feet above. He fastened his shotgun to his belt and, opening his knife, began cutting horizontal notches in the cliff side for hand and toe holds. He chipped his notches slanting in and downward so that he would not slip. Trouble began when he was six feet above the quag. Hanging to the cliff side by one foot and one hand, as he gouged his notches, put an increasing strain on his muscles. He had to cut a new notch for his other hand each time before releasing an aching arm or foot. Added to this the rain began suddenly again. It beat upon his back and soon made each hand and foothold slippery and precarious.

He looked down after a bit and what he saw made his blue eyes harden. Involuntarily he clung closer to the cliff side. Five or six alligators were churning about at the base of the cliff, drawn irresistibly by the scent of live meat. Their heads lifted and turned from side to side in fierce expectance as they gazed at the man above. One monster, with jaws and head broader than Mayhew's square-thewed thorax, reared against the cliff side with hollow echoing snarls. The teeth in his vast, crooked jaws were yellowed snags. His round-knobbed nostrils opened and closed as he tested the air, blowing twin blasts of foul air through them. The green eyes were slit like a goat's and glared up at Mayhew with a sort of devilish understanding. He reared until his gaping jaws were no more than three feet below the man. Then the mouth snapped shut, became a thin, wet, crooked seam, from which a prolonged hissing sound came forth.

Even in his precarious plight Mayhew found little pockets of time to marvel at the size of this monster and experience a collector's regret that such a specimen could not be taken out to prove to the world that such dragons really existed. The creatures were as calm and inexorable in their purpose as this land that had spawned them, as nature itself. There was no added challenge or glare of eye at the propinquity of their hoped-for prey, no added bluff, hate or ferocity in the fact that the tender meal clinging to the cliff side was a human being—the two-legged lord of creation. They simply slavered for warm and living meat, and this food they had followed was obviously more tantalizing and easier to kill than anything to be caught in their regular swampy ways.

Mayhew cut his next notch deeper and at an even more pronounced angle, and beside it he cut another, for in a matter of minutes he would have to rest both hands and feet for a space because of the unnatural strain on his muscles. He gained the double handhold at last, switched his weight to the other foot with a kicking motion, and became almost bold with relief as the aches of his body eased. He had only to be cautious now to be safe, he thought, and felt like shouting aloud, and in that instant catastrophe almost overtook him. The single wet handhold he had been clinging to suddenly crumbled; earth and rock slithered down upon him, almost unbalancing him, and but for his new handhold he would have plunged downward to those waiting jaws below. A bedlam of snarling and snapping came from down there as the shower of earth roused the muggers to fresh anticipation.

The rain had begun to weaken the surface earth, or else Mayhew was reaching a portion of the cliff where the formation was more crumbly. Again sweat stood out on his body as he braced himself desperately against the cliff in an endeavor to take the weight off hands and feet, and he hacked with his knife at a new hold.

Darkness was not far off. He looked upward along a slope as steep as a church spire. The small outcropping tree was still twenty-five feet above him. Some fifty feet farther up vines and jungle growth showed; doubtless a plateau, trees and safety lay up there, but his goal now was the little tree.

The minutes that followed were tense and desperate labor and filled with a concentration like prayer. Once again a handhold crumpled beneath his weight; and, balanced precariously on one foot, fighting down vertigo, he had to gouge a fresh one. At last he was able to grip the base of the jutting tree. Small as it was, it held, and he drew himself up and across it.

The rain had ceased again; darkness had fallen. For the time being Mayhew was safe. But he did not fancy his position. The muggers would wait indefinitely; they would prowl and return. The only way out was still up.

Jungle sounds came from above him—they had been

going on for some time, he realized, but he had been too occupied to pay heed—weird squallings, hissings and swishings. Jungle cats, beyond a doubt—either panther or "tiger" as the natives called the jaguar. A treacherous customer, the jaguar, addicted to the bad habit of wrapping himself about the human neck via some overhanging tree branch. Tiger above him, dragons below.

He was exhausted, drained of energy and nerve force. He was in for a night of it on the cliff side and it would be a long one. With his knife he fell to chipping out a hole above the little tree, large enough for his hips and thighs, so he could lean back and rest. Once this was done, he gouged out a further shelf for his pack and gun. He wondered wryly as he worked, if Colombia, not satisfied with hiding its treasure from him, would not let him even escape. He decided he would certainly escape next day. A dreamy analgesia wrapped about him as his muscles began to relax. . . .

He awoke with a violent start, his body sagging sidewise into giddy space. Shaking, he gripped the tree, fighting off his drugged exhaustion. He could not afford to doze again without tying himself to the tree. But there was nothing to tie himself with.

Down below in the mist and blackness, sounds arose as from a fen. The muggers were still on watch. Mayhew ate the bit of food that remained in his pack and began to chip again at the cliff side above the tree. If he persisted, he might hew out a niche large enough for safe sleeping. After an hour he had achieved a sizable hole and dozed again.

With the dawn he heard again the hissing, squalling sounds of jaguar from the jungle above. He began his climb at once, cutting his ladder of notches in the cliff side in a line directly above the little tree. If he should slip again and fall, the tree might save him. But this day was to be wholly different from the preceding. The rain held off through the morning hours. The mists lifted above the jungle roof and for minutes the sun shone through as if nature were smiling. Now Mayhew's ladder rose steadily and without mishap. The way, as he climbed, became easier and less steep.

Toward noon he reached the top of the rampart. A jungled plateau stretched away before him, and his hand gripped a trailing liana that meant safety. He could have shouted for joy, but he repressed the impulse, refrained from even moving, for directly ahead of him he heard again the hissing spitting sound of jaguar. And Mayhew had seen rather too much of the Colombian jaguar.

He clung where he was, peering through the green. He saw a pair of rare black umbrella birds, the "crows" of the Colombian natives. They were scolding at something they saw in the depths of a tree. Mayhew could see them filling their strange air sacs, bright scarlet pouches the size of tomatoes. When the sac was distended a peculiar squalling sound was produced. It was when the air was expelled from the sac that a swishing sound, closely resembling the spitting of a big cat, filled the air. Mayhew burst out in spontaneous but silent laughter over the jaguars with which his imagination had peopled the wood. And then he saw what the "crows" were scolding.

A flame-red bird rose from the depths of the tree and planed silently away into the bush—a black-winged bird with a body of the indescribable color of incandescent metal just before it reaches white heat. Flame-red even to its head, a very flame alive. The Fird Bird, cock-of-the-rock—prize and despair of scientists, which Mayhew had trailed for fifty days, beginning to doubt its existence. But there it was.

As the "crows" lifted and followed the fiery one, Mayhew climbed onto the lush plateau and followed the "crows." He came after a time to a Cecropia wood where seven or eight of the birds fed like flame-flowers among the trees.

Exultation surged through the man as he lay in the thickets and watched. Into his lungs he inhaled great breaths in a spreading, swelling rush of thanks and gladness. This was his jungle strike, his precious fleece, and like that Jason of old, he had had to pass dragons to find it.

The rest, the catching of his specimens, would be a matter of old routine. He would return with native helpers and his equipment. For days, perhaps weeks, he would study the habits of the birds, then set his pocket nets in the likeliest places. In the end he would win; he was given to know that infallibly as he began his trek back to his base camp, around the flank of the mountain. He read it in the air, in the different bird calls and some subtle change that had come over the face of the jungle. From years in the open, Mayhew could read such things almost as an animal might. It was as if Colombia, having made her tests and tried him well, had deigned to smile at last.

▪ The Blasted Pine

NOVEMBER HAD LAID ITS MELANCHOLY HUSH OVER THE FAR northern valley of the Kinnebec. The bare-branched hardwoods along the slopes made delicate tracery against the marble skies, and the winds coursing down from the rocky ramparts at the valley's head whispered eerily of imminent snow.

Toward the end of a gloomy afternoon a curious-looking animal might have been seen making his way down the valley, coming from the heavy spruce forests to the north. The newcomer was a giant wolverine, a creature who seems predestined for evil, whose fangs and claws are against every other dweller of the wilderness. The various other names he went by—Injun devil, carcajou, glutton and bad dog— were each an epithet coming from a different tongue, expressing ultimate loathing. Ishmael would have been another, equally appropriate, for his arrant genius for deviltry and destruction has made this little beast the most thoroughly hated creature that prowls.

Though it was broad daylight, the newcomer progressed with a total unconcern, keeping to the open places as nothing but the lordly moose and the black bear ever venture to do. His movement was a curious double shuffle, a swagger full of truculent assurance, though as to size he was under three feet in length. But wise as he was beyond all the other creatures of the wild, and of a savage ferocity which few would dare to cross even if his musky flesh were appetizing, which it was not, he had good reason to loaf before the mightiest he knew.

Ishmael was the largest and fiercest member of the *Mustelidae* family, which includes the weasels, minks, martens, and all the professional assassins of the wilderness world. Ishmael inherited the worst elements of all his unsavory ancestors, and the fine qualities of none, unless one counted his courage. He had courage, as all things must which live outside the law. For the rest, he was surlier than a badger, more odious than any skunk, and more ferocious even, for his size, than the fisher marten, his first cousin. A fox was stupid beside him, and he possessed a strength greater for his weight than any other living beast.

Some perversion of his hybrid nature inspires this little beast wantonly to rob, destroy and make trouble with fiendish ingenuity in all his encounters with other creatures, yet there is no experienced trapper but will admit that he is the most wily and efficient of all the forest marauders.

Ishmael was at present in search of a new hunting range, nor had he any scruple as to poaching upon the preserves of others. In all such matters he was a law unto himself. The gloomy valley of the Kinnebec, with its dark ravines mantled with spruce, appealed to him. Here the dense, century-old growth of evergreens excluded all sunlight; the tangled windfalls of a valley bottom made a labyrinth of lairs, runways and ambushes. Through the perpetual twilight beneath the spruce he moved like a spirit of the place, his black ominous head low hung and swinging. Ishmael's gait more than anything else epitomized the malign nature of him. He lurched like a swagman on his short thick legs, and his back kept arching with the sinister undulations of a measuring worm.

That night the carcajou slept in a hole in the top of an ancient stump. He did not take the trouble to keep an ear cocked for danger, for his evil reputation made even the cougar and the wolf, his most dangerous enemies, think long before disputing ground with him. Having thus formally taken over the district, his inordinate appetite had him stirring in the cold black hour before the dawn to exact a tribute. By nature he was a night prowler, but his long migration had thrown him temporarily out of his nocturnal bent. Up along the spruce-grown slope of the valley he drifted as the gray began to waver in the east. His soundless penetration of the tangled thickets was a marvel and a diablerie for so squat and logy a form, but his entire resource lay in this amazing craft and stealth.

Presently in the black shadows of a juniper thicket he almost stepped on something warm that stirred. A beast of any other persuasion would have leaped back in a momentary start, but the wolverine had not even an instant's recoil. With no perceptible pause his fangs buried themselves in the throat of the tiny spotted fawn that lay there. Though his nose was second to no living thing's in keenness, it had given him no warning, for in the first few weeks of life the fawn has no scent.

Only one broken bleat of terror marked the slaying as Ishmael's powerful jaws met in the baby's neck. Crouched above his prey, Ishmael remained for a moment moveless. If the mother deer happened to be near, her infuriated rush might prove dangerous even to him, but in this instance the doe had wandered far.

Ishmael drank deep of the warm blood, after which he

settled down like the trencherman he was, to the process
of packing as much solid meat into his system as it could
hold without bursting. The mere slaking of his hunger
pangs was negligible in this beast's hunting; he lived for
gluttony, prolonged orgies of gorging and the deep feeding
dreams which followed.

As he was licking his black lips with omnivorous satisfaction over the repast, a stirring in the nearby thicket froze
him to the fixity of stone. He glared in the direction of the
sound, but instead of the vengeful mother of the fawn, a
great black head emerged from the undergrowth, swaying
cumbrously from side to side as its owner tested the breeze.
It was a full-grown she-bear of an extraordinary size, and
the sight of her brought the carcajou's lips twitching up
from his teeth. This particular she-bear was his specific and
deadly enemy, and he had thought her many miles away to
the north. She had reason to remember him as well. Only
two months before he had dispatched her single cub, whom
he found playing alone in a sunny glade, afterward nar-
rowly escaping the old mother's wrath.

The smell of the fresh blood reached the bear's keen nose.
With the time for hibernating close at hand she was in great
need of rich, strong feeding to sustain her through the winter months. She came straight on, and for a moment the rage
of the carcajou was so great that it almost seemed to efface
the disparity of their statures. Then he did that which more
than anything else illustrated his diabolic nature: he be-
fouled the carcass of the fawn with the vile-smelling musk
from his scent bag.

The nose of the bear brought back the old association
and she flung herself savagely forward. But ten feet ahead
of her the wolverine turned and slipped like a shadow into
the undergrowth. His enemy fell upon the kill and tore a

piece from the carcass to set her brand of possession upon it. But that mouthful was never swallowed. Though the fawn's meat would have been a godsend to the bear at this time, the overpowering reek of carcajou nauseated her. No other living thing could eat of that meat now, and the carcajou knew it well. To have the meat snatched from her in so vile and indirect a manner loosed a raging demon in the old bear. She pivoted about on her hind quarters and flung away on the wolverine's trail.

But the few moments gained had been ample time for Ishmael's wily brain to light on a clever ruse. Two hundred feet away he came upon an ancient blowdown, uprooted by a long-ago storm, its dead bulk leaning against one of its living neighbors. Part of its shattered top overhung a rocky ravine which dropped thirty feet to the tops of the evergreens below. Up the leaning bole Ishmael clambered, and near the top splatted himself flat to wait. In two minutes the she-bear emerged from the thicket hot on his trail and, sighting the despoiler in the topmost crotch, instantly started climbing. The dead conifer trembled under her weight; the carcajou dug his claws into the trunk and bared his teeth in soundless menace. He knew what he must do now and he was ready, but still in no hurry. The farther the bear mounted the trunk the better. Finally when she was but a few feet below him, he steadied himself, then launched downward into space.

It was a desperate feat, yet he had done it many times before in a similar predicament. Claws widespread he crashed sprawling into the tops of the spruce below, and as he struck, his powerful forelegs clutched the branches with all his strength. The tough resilient limbs bent almost double as he slithered down among them, but they did not break. He dropped the last fifteen feet to the ground amidst a shower of broken twigs, unhurt except for a cut in his hide beneath the right foreleg.

On the ground he crouched motionless, listening, until silence pervaded the forest once more. He had hoped the bear might hurl herself after him and dash herself to pieces, but mad as she was she was not rash enough for that. He was safe for the time.

Through the confusion of the windfalls he picked a twisty course with a cunning he knew would put the bear to the limit of her skill to follow; then he sought a cleft in the rocks to rest and lick his bruises. The appearance of his enemy somewhat blighted the outlook on his new range, but he knew that soon she would be forced to hole up and leave him a free agent for the winter months.

Next day the first of the November snows came sifting through the pines. It was dusk on this day when the wolverine caught his first glimpse of his other and more dangerous enemies of the valley, of whose existence he had not dreamed. Searching for a winter den, he saw two men upon the slope above him. Noiseless as a shadow the carcajou slipped after them, drawn by an equal fear and fascination, intent on studying the men and marking the place where they dwelt. Hate was written on his black face and in his glowering eyes. Craftily he dogged their footsteps, unknown and unseen. Once the woodsmen both stopped and stood motionless, peering back with an intuitive sense of being followed. But the carcajou stopped at the same instant, masking himself in the thickets.

To the very edge of the woodmen's clearing he followed, led by his malign curiosity. There he flattened himself beneath a low balsam and watched until the men had closed their door for the night. He circled the cabin then, familiarizing himself with the scent of his enemies, imprinting upon his consciousness all the details of the clearing. To his way of thinking, these two men were simply interlopers upon a promising range which belonged rightly to him, and then and there he set himself to devising means by which their life here would be made intolerable.

The Wyant brothers, Eben and Jude, had built their split-log cabin at the head of the Kinnebec Valley. Ostensibly the brothers were backwoods farmers; they had cleared a meager two acres, fought the stumps and stones, and each year planted corn and potatoes. But all this was mere summer makeshift for the Wyants. These lank woodsmen were true sons of the wilderness; life for them didn't really begin till fall set in and they took up the activities of the trap line and the hunting trail.

It was on the morning after the wolverine had followed them home that the brothers began laying several trapping lines for the winter months. The lines ran along the densely wooded valley bottom and up the larger ravines. The utmost craft was used in their setting. Among the tangled blowdowns they devised clever snares and deadfalls of logs which often proved more efficient than the best of traps. The light fall of snow which had begun the day before continued and worked into their hands that day, obliterating all tracks. But it worked into the hands of the small slouching form that followed them as well.

For all unknown to them Ishmael had that morning taken up his agreeable game of shadowing again. He had seen the brothers leave their cabin and had followed at a discreet distance to see what they were about. Eyes bright with malign sagacity, Ishmael was a witness to all their movements that morning, and a growing satisfaction began to be blended with the little animal's hate. He knew traps from many a firsthand experience, and to such as he a trap was a boon, not a menace—often turning up a double banquet, the bait and the baited.

All that day the Wyants kept diligently at their work setting out a fifteen-mile area, and until midday the old wolverine dogged their footsteps. Then he sought a hollow tree and slept, to be abroad again with the night.

Toward dusk, as the brothers were climbing out of a gloomy ravine in the valley bottom, an ancient half-dead pine called their attention by its great size. It was a hoary monarch of its kind, a couple of centuries old, and the only remnant of its day left in the region. Old rotting stumps showed how some long-ago fire had demolished its fellows. The bark was beginning to fall away in patches and half its boughs were bare and dead. A great hollow at its base showed the inroad many a fire had made into its heart.

The Wyants knelt and peered up into the dark hollow bole, ever alert to discover some new secret of the forest. Jude, the younger, unslung a marten set and was preparing to plant it in the opening, when his brother's hand restrained him.

"Bear tree," Eben said. "Let be. We'll take a look at it again, come January."

Jude nodded.

"Bear'll hole up early this year," Eben predicted. "No mast. Sol Wire seen one over on the shoulder last week—hunger proud, asuckin' his paws."

The snow had begun to fall intermittently again as Ishmael went humping and slouching along the valley bottom that night. He was in search of a meal with a seasoning of devilish amusement thrown in, and he knew where the combination could be most easily found: along the Wyants' fresh-laid trap lines. In a ravine he came presently upon a marten set carefully buried in the brush and snow. He placed it to an inch, by the smell of iron that came up to him. Then he craftily dug about it, uncovered the chain, and fell to jerking it until the trap finally sprung, as he knew it would. His lips lifted and flickered as if in derision, as he squatted and devoured the bait.

Not satisfied with this, he vented his mean nature on the trap itself, entangling it in the brush so that half an hour of vexatious work would be necessary to unsnarl it. Then he passed on.

He came presently upon a weasel trap with a fresh-killed victim. A few brief minutes were occupied in tearing his tiny cousin from the trap and bolting him. Then he wrenched the trap from its fastenings and disappeared with it into the gloom of the forest. That trap was never found again.

The carcajou covered twenty miles that night in his depredations, and hardly a trap, snare or deadfall on the Wyants' line but was robbed, demolished or dragged away and buried, as his whim dictated. When daylight came he was curled up asleep on a rocky ledge.

That afternoon the Wyants covered the territory they had set out, and when they met at dusk at the farthest limit of their lines each had a sulphurous story to tell of the havoc that had been wrought.

"Injun devil," Jude muttered, and his brother nodded.

Nettled as they were over their losses, their wrath was not untempered with a degree of pleasure at the prospect of the game that loomed ahead. They set themselves at once to planning schemes of reprisal for the succeeding days.

"The varmint's old and wise," Eben said. "Git him at his own game, we will. Keep on asetting bait for a spell as if we thought we'd wear him down, then plant double sets, one with bait and one without. That ought to fetch him."

As the brothers turned homeward they talked in low tones of the plans for the morrow, stopping to reset the traps and snares that were not made useless by the carcajou.

"Think there might be two of them?" Jude asked.

"Two nothing! Ain't room in the woods for two o' him!" Eben said.

They talked like injured men, but a grim satisfaction grew upon them at the increasing evidence of the wolverine's sagacity. To Jude, at least, the prospect of a prolonged contest with the wiliest of all the forest dwellers was more edifying than the richest harvest of furs, for it helped to lift the unconscious loneliness and monotony of their forest life.

For a week thereafter the curious feud between the two men and the small quadruped continued, with the score of vantage continually mounting in favor of the wolverine.

The end of two weeks found the brothers sitting by their daubed clay fireplace finishing some final preparations against the little robber who by now had usurped their every waking thought. Six traps had been burned in the open fire to destroy every scent of iron or human hands. They handled the traps with mittens which had been treated with a solution of lye. Today they were to supplement each main set with a second unbaited trap.

That afternoon they made the rounds, using infinite care to preserve the unsullied appearance of the snow about each set. Early dusk that night found the old Injun devil abroad as usual, traversing the valley bottom in a particularly evil frame of mind. He had not slept well that day, and it was high time he found himself a permanent den against the growing cold.

Tonight as he approached the trap lines he exercised a greater caution than ever before, seemingly warned by an uncanny presage of the new menace awaiting him. Along the line were the fresh-made tracks of the Wyants' snowshoes, with which he now insolently blended his own, for he had become negligent on the matter of harm coming to him from the men themselves. But that careful camouflaging of the snow about the sets did not fool him.

The first set he came to he robbed of two goodly chunks of frozen fish without mishap. A bit farther on the scent of dead grouse made him lick his muzzle hungrily. Beneath a spreading larch tree he viewed a curious-looking bark shelter built against the tree to keep the snow from the trap. Within the opening lay the grouse in a bed of feathers. Ishmael knew that danger lurked about so tempting a banquet. He circled the layout, studying it with savage eyes, and finally began an inch-by-inch approach, delicately testing every inch of the snow before putting his foot upon it. No smell of iron came to him until he was a foot away. The trap lay in the opening of the shelter. Cunningly he dug down to the chain, and in another minute the whole set lay uncovered. Carefully he pulled the thing aside, then scooped the dead bird into the open with a flick of his paw.

Almost at the same instant he leaped into the air with a calamitous squall of pain. Spinning round as he lighted, he tore desperately at the two steel jaws that had seized upon one hind foot in a deathly clamp.

For a moment panic ran down the dim aisles of the woods as the thief, bent double, whirled about in a mad fight to break the awful thing that clutched his foot. He clawed at it wildly, but the contraption held.

As there was obviously nothing to be gained by his frenzied efforts, Ishmael grew suddenly calm with a return of the cold, deadly acumen that made him what he was. He sat down in the snow and set his wits to work. If violent movement would not do it, try deliberate twists, reasoning out each move. For a long time he worked, but the steel teeth were inexorable.

There was a final recourse, a last desperate measure: to turn his own jaws upon the imprisoned foot. It would take all his stoic courage but without flinching he proceeded; chewing through his own flesh and gristle and at last pulling free. Two toes had to be left behind him in the trap.

His predilection for trouble momentarily gone, Ishmael limped away, leaving a bloody trail. Toward the remote end of the valley he made his way, and before dawn came he found the sanctuary for which he sought. Among the tangled windfalls, relics of other centuries, one ancient pine tree still stood. At its base was a great hollow that ran up into the bole. Three feet up in the black interior he found a perfectly ordained shelf in the punky wood just large enough for him to curl up on. There, protected from the cold and wind, he fell into a deep healing sleep.

On the following day the Wyants viewed with a mixture of satisfaction and chagrin the near success of their stratagem.

"Pinched his toes for fair, that time," Eben said.

They studied the bloody signs in the snow.

"Try trackin' him," Eben said. "He'll hole up for a spell to heal."

They followed the blood-marked trail, but within an hour lost it completely in the hopeless tangle of the windfalls.

Throughout the week Ishmael remained curled up in his hollow tree while the clean air and prolonged sleep performed their healing work. The fifth day saw the flesh and sinews of his foot knit once more, though the remaining toes had fallen away and the smooth stump of his leg bone

protruded. He would always limp but his imdomitable
courage and arrogance were dampened not a whit. When
he walked forth at the end of a week it was, if possible, in
a still more indurated spirit of deviltry.

Craving strong rich food he made straight for the
Wyants' trap lines. At trap after trap he stopped to stuff
himself with meat. After his capacity had been reached he
continued the rounds for the mere saturnalia of ruin he was
able to wreak.

So involved was he in his game that he lingered on well
into the morning. Suddenly, the dry crunching of the snow
heralded the approach of the Wyants, and he tarried to
watch them. As it happened, the catch of the night before
had been the richest of the season. Not only had Ishmael
avoided every snare they had planted for him, but his work
of destruction had been complete.

No talk was wasted between the brothers as they turned
homeward to prepare for a relentless hunt. Ishmael, from
his covert, watched them go.

Sometime later as he was nearing his hollow tree for a
day's sleep, he suddenly stopped short in the blowdowns
to test the breeze. A sharp but indefinable warning had impressed his superacute senses, coming how or from where
it could not be said. For no definite reason he changed his
idea of sleeping and continued on down the valley, moving
at his best limping pace. He did not suspect that less than
a mile behind him the Wyants were gliding along on his
fresh trail on their ten-foot whispering skis, on which they
had more than once run down a fleeing fox. At first he did
not suspect it. Then, though the wind was against him, an
intimation came. It was a faint sound that came to him as
Jude made a flying jump, a kind of *chug* and a soft tearing
slither. Soon afterward he had a fleeting glimpse of his trail-

ers as they flitted across the open space far to the rear. A low
thick hiss came from the carcajou and thereafter he climbed
whenever he could, and kept climbing, with an instinctive
knowledge of the vantage gained.

The time that the Wyants lost climbing out of the valley
was quickly regained along the windswept ridges. The third
hour almost saw the finish of the desperate game. As the
carcajou shuffled along a rock ledge, lips flecked with foam
from his tremendous exertions, there came a skimming
flight as of birds as the two men swept after him on the
downgrade. Ishmael whirled, then flung himself blindly
over the rocky ledge into space, and the quick-aimed bullets
went wild as the hunters flashed by. Ishmael hurtled downward forty feet onto another snowy ledge, bounced over it
and went bounding down until he was lost to sight in the
shadows of the young evergreens that choked the gorge below. The Wyants loved life better than he, for they did not
attempt to follow.

Once more they were forced to turn homeward empty-
handed.

Ishmael, from the opposite side of the valley, had watched
them go, and then doggedly set out after them, his goal
being no less than his home tree.

That night the wind increased steadily and by midnight
the temperature had fallen twenty degrees. Ishmael's re-
pose was troubled by many unaccustomed forest noises as
the gale played havoc around him. His own tree swayed and
groaned deep down in its fibers as the blasts tugged at its
mighty roots. The once iron heart of the old pine was soft
and riven from the ravages of a half century of decay and
a myriad of boring insects.

The clock of the wilderness timed the end just a few min-

utes after Ishmael emerged the following morning in answer
to the spur of his empty stomach—and with a deep-laid purpose. A fusillade of mighty snappings from the overwrought
wood ran through the forest like a volley of rifle fire as the
fibers at the giant's base began to part; the two-hundred-
foot crown swayed and staggered. Then with an inanimate
moaning sound the monarch careened and fell crashing.

The far-reaching thunder of its final descent caught Ishmael in his tracks a quarter of a mile down the valley, and
he left off eating a captured grouse to listen. In its fall the
giant roots of the pine had torn up an excavation in the
earth, big as a bomb pit. Presently, among the tangled roots
and earth, a startling movement might have been seen. It
was as if the great scar in the earth were given birth to an
apparition, as a gaunt old female bear emerged from the hole
—none other than Ishmael's old-time enemy.

Weeks before, at the beginning of the first snow, the she-
bear had come upon the blasted pine as had Ishmael, and
chosen it for her winter hibernation. Deep down among the
roots below ground, she had dug a den for herself, and the
end of the first month of her mysterious sleep had found her
covered over with a blanket of drifted snow some two feet
thick. When Ishmael had chosen the hollow tree for sanctuary some two months later, the winter storms had effec-
tively covered every trace and scent of the sleeping occu-
pant.

The great tree's fall had partially uncovered the bear's
den, and it had been the ruthless sting of the knife-edged
wind that finally roused her from her deathlike torpor. Her
rest had been poor at best. Thanks to Ishmael, her almost
human sorrowing over her murdered cub had worn her
thin in the fall, and she had failed to put on the necessary

blanket of fat against the long sleep. Now that her den had been destroyed she was doomed to wander homeless and miserable, seeking what scanty sustenance could be found in the winter woods till spring broke the clamp of famine. Knowledge of this, combined with her rude awakening, had roused the old she-bear to a demoniac rage. No sooner had she emerged from her hole than she came upon the fresh trail of Ishmael, the creature she had to come to hate above all living things.

A low rumbling note of anger issued from deep down in the old mother's chest as she stood, head swaying, testing the wind. Gaunt as a specter, she looked like the spirit of vengeance as she swung about and shambled away on the trail Ishmael had left.

About half an hour later Ishmael himself returned, coming from the opposite direction. A vague sense of something wrong prompted caution as he approached the spot, and the appalling sight of the great conifer lying prone along the hillside gripped him for a minute in a spell of awe and terror. Then he came upon the fresh tracks of the she-bear. The hair rose stiffly along his spine at the familiar, frightening scent.

Along the prostrate trunk of the great pine he shambled, savage, bewildered. Except that it had fallen the tree seemed still intact. There was the hollow at its base, easy of access and a good sanctuary still. It was as he was peering within that the old she-bear emerged from the woods scarcely a hundred feet distant. Before she had made him out Ishmael slipped quickly into the hollow of the bole. The hole, he knew, was too small to admit of her great bulk.

Soon the body of the old mother darkened the hole opening. Her nose told her Ishmael was within, and grimly, relentlessly she set to work tearing her way into his retreat.

That night the Wyant brothers sat talking by their fire, conversation as usual pivoting around the evil little genius, when mention was made of the hollow pine they had discovered early in the fall. As they talked a conviction began to grow upon them that they had hit upon the secret of the old carcajou's winter retreat.

The first light found them traversing the valley bottom on their snowshoes. The storm had abated in the night. When they searched the sky line for the towering crown of the king pine that had formerly stood out as a landmark, and found it gone, they doubled their pace. It was not long before they were standing beside the fallen monarch, wordless as they deciphered the intricate story written in the snow. Down by the roots of the tree they found a flattened furry form, torn, battered and literally shredded into strips all that was left of Ishmael, the indomitable. Round about were signs of a battle that had been waged with a bear—a beast at least fifteen times his size and weight, and those signs told of no one-sided fray. The trail of the bear that led down the valley was marked by carmine splashes.

"They fought," Jude said, in something like awe, and either brother would have given his finest pelt to have witnessed the thing. "The little critter was cornered in the hole, an' lit into the bear at the end, like a nest of red devils!"

The thing that puzzled them was the reason back of the bear's relentless fury.

"Musta had a grudge agin him, like ourselves," Eben said. "He's done for, but it's no credit to us. He had us fair stumped at every turn of the game; I'll give that to him, the little cuss, an' he was the one critter of the woods that could of done it. Reckon he went out with full honors, too, for his size."

Something of the same mystical fancy that makes the far northern Indians covet a garment of carcajou fur as an aid to craft and bravery prompted Jude's remark:

"Got me a job to do, 'fore I'm done with trapping. Ketch me a prime devil fur."

▪ Deer Slayer

THOUGH THE WIND HAD NOT SHIFTED, THE COPPERY HAZE that hid the sun seemed thinning a bit, the air less strangling. The two cougars, slinking belly down along a jagged game trail slackened their flight. The horror in their lambent gooseberry eyes was lessening and from time to time they paused to get the feel of the new region about them.

They had traveled twenty-four hours without food or rest through new country fraught with unknown danger. For five years they had made their home among those distant mountains to the east, where with the eagles they had been overlords of fifty miles of tumbled peaks and valleys. Then, all within an hour, had come the inexplicable terror of the forest fire, which could neither be fought nor endured.

At first it had been but a yellow haze veiling the sky; then a terrifying odor began to permeate the air, smarting the membranes of the nose and eyes. It had set the cougar pair pacing restlessly back and forth on the rocky ledge that fronted their den. By midafternoon the sunlight was gone; the mountain slopes were bathed in a lurid light like the end of the world, and a furtive panic ran through all the forest world. As the cougars paced and turned five deer broke sud-

denly from cover a few hundred yards below them and
went bounding away to the west, eyes distended, nostrils
flaring.

The deer had hardly disappeared when a pair of gray
foxes slipped by. Pausing momentarily to look behind them,
they melted into the thickets, bellies down in desperate
speed. Innumerable rabbits, marmots, and chipmunks were
likewise streaking through the undergrowth and running
among them an occasional mink or weasel, wholly oblivious
of natural enemies.

All this panic was communicated to the cougars, but
they, last of all gave way to flight. Nocturnal in their habits
they wanted to hide in the dark recess of their den; likewise they had the cat tribe's aversion to travel. They whined
as they paced, but not until the sound of the fire was in the
air, like the roar of surf on a distant shore, did they join the
general flight.

From the top of a distant crag they turned to watch fascinated as the flames licked up the trees all round the rocky
pinnacle upon which they had dwelt for years. Thereafter
the pair had bent their every energy to putting miles behind
them. Now toward sunset they found themselves at the
head of the wild tumbling valley of the Miramichi, far beyond reach of the fire.

From a pinnacle of rock they surveyed the surrounding
valleys in the blue dusk. The scene below was eloquent of
solitude and the vesper song of canyon wrens only made
the stillness more complete. Presently both cats dropped to
the ground and melted into the shadows beneath the low
spruce trees.

For a time all that was to be seen of them were four
greenish moons as the two beasts threaded the dark. They
put all their craft in their stalking that night. Having found

a well-frequented deer trail, the big male climbed to a high
pine bough overhanging the run and waited, while the female circled far to drive the deer toward him down the
wind.

Instead of a pair or two of weathered and wary bucks
foraging alone, as was the usual thing at this time of summer, the she-cougar started up a mixed band of six animals.
As they milled together stamping and snoofing the lioness
was among them, cruel claws slashing, white fangs agleam.
Her initial spring landed her upon the shoulders of a big
buck; one forepaw hooked beneath his neck in the dislo-
cating wrench which was her favorite way of killing, and
before the herd had wholly scattered she made a second
kill by launching herself upon a plunging young doe and
ripping out her throat. The killer bounded free, lifting up
her voice in an indescribable yell of savagery and blood lust
that brought her mate bounding up the slope. It was the
kill cry of the cougar kind that was soon to be heard nightly
along those forested slopes and valleys.

For a long time the pair fed upon the fresh venison, drink-
ing deeply of the warm blood to restore their spent tissues.
Later, as the moon climbed above the pine spires, they found
a den in which to sleep off their blood drunk—a cavelike
fissure in the face of a jutting cliff. Hidden from above, it
was approachable only by a narrow shelf of rock which
none but a goat or a cat could navigate.

It was a natural stronghold wholly to their liking. They
slept—the long deep recuperative sleep which the tense
springs of their organisms required. When they awakened
next day it was with a sense of well-being and growing
proprietorship.

They had intended to feed again on the kills of the night
before, but even as they ate the chance of a fresh kill came

—a warm scent in the dark that told of deer feeding below. The big male, a shadow among denser shadows, crouched a moment, then leaped. A few minutes later came the broken cry of a deer and the kill cry of the lion.

Again they fed upon meat still warm, something like awe in their savage brains at the ease of the hunting in this new range. They could not know, of course, that they had come into one of the government's game preserves where all browsing animals had thriven and multiplied during twenty years of guardianship. Having fed and drunk deeply at a sidehill spring, they spent the remainder of the night covering the region in ever-widening circles. For the next week they continued their tours of investigation, establishing themselves as they went by deed and reputation as the overlords of the district.

Luck continued to favor them in whatever direction they hunted. Game seemed limitless, game moreover which showed complete ignorance of the cougars' sinister ways. Back on their old range they had been lucky to kill a deer a week. Now, night after night, both cats killed, simply because the chance presented itself and in their blood was the memory of much privation.

Gradually the sense of well-being and dominance grew upon them. Their hunting took them farther and farther afield. They were remarkable and terrible killing machines, the big male measuring nine feet from the tip of his tail to his black whiskers. In all the high country there were no hunters but would give them the trail. They conquered the low-lying valleys as they had conquered the heights, and an insufferable arrogance grew in them.

In their sheltered existence in this natural park the browsers had long depended upon their eyes as their truest safeguard. Hence none were inclined to flee at an unfamiliar

scent and the cougars could approach almost to springing
distance of their prey so long as they did not show themselves. Stalking became a form of play, rather than a necessity. Often they hunted for the sheer pleasure of killing,
leaving the bulk of their kill for the meatbirds and other
undertakers of the forest.

Within a month, true to feline nature, they had turned
into a pair of tyrants whose rule was the rule of fear and
death and who knew no moderation. Nightly they voiced
their triumphs—harsh coughing wauls that echoed across
the still, mountain-girt valleys, and froze in their tracks all
lesser creatures of the thickets.

Summer drew into fall with little change in the prodigal
state of affairs. The cougars had come to love the new life
past any telling. Their memory was short-lived and they
had all but forgotten they had ever known want. At the beginning of the first fall snows the elk bands began to drift
through the mountain passes toward the west. Here was
new game to the cougars. The elk scent drew the killers
forth one afternoon in broad daylight, and from the top of
a ridge they watched flame-eyed the first stately herds
winding their way over the divide.

For a space both cats were awed at the size and majesty of
these tall stalking creatures which marched steadily forward
looking neither to the right nor the left. But soon the warm
rich scent overruled that. The cougars melted from sight
in the sparse pine trees that furred the ridge. When next
they showed it was as if they had leaped out of the ground
in the very midst of the herd.

The voice of a bull elk was lifted in a hoarse bugling roar.
The roar choked into sobbing coughs, followed hard by
sounds as of a stampede which died away in the distance,
interspersed with bleating bellows. Finally two cat screams

split the breeze. Then silence, and along the high valley floor, all within a mile, three carcasses of full-grown elk lay strewn in grotesque attitudes of death. All had been killed in full flight by dislocation of the neck, the cougars having ridden each victim to death, bounding free of one pitching body to fasten leechlike to the back of another.

That night the high country stillness was troubled by the wails and yappings of coyotes from the lowlands bickering over the kills. And with the dawn the scavengers still tarried, dividing their quarreling among an increasing flock of meatbirds, while in their den nearby the cougars stirred uneasily in their blood-drunken sleep, and not alone because of the sounds without.

They had departed from the protective routine of normality. A saturnalia of killing such as they had set in motion was necessarily hazardous and short-lived, and nature, who fosters no monsters for all her seeming ruthlessness, was already moving to correct the situation. The crows, jays, and buzzards, flocking for a hundred miles round to the feast, black specks against the cloudless sky, were the dots and dashes of her Morse code, flashing a message for the eyes of the world.

It was no later than the following afternoon that the cougar pair, who had killed and hunted for six years unhampered, discovered that they were being hunted in turn. They were stealing forth before their usual hour to wreak more havoc among the elk bands when they crossed the fresh trail of a man.

At the sharp human scent which stood for their one dangerous enemy, the ears of both cats were plastered flat against their skulls in instinctive defiance. Guilt and instinct whispered that the man was on their own trail. Their long dog fangs bared in a sullen rage.

Because of that new trail their hunting that night was sketchy, and for the first time on the new range their kill cry was not raised, for many of their favorite trails were redolent with the touch and presence of the new enemy. Long before their usual hour they were back in their den for the day.

Dave Baxter, park game warden, was tired, packsore and out of sorts. For a week now he had been in the open, tracking with dogged persistence the pair of newcomers in his preserve, whose ways were the ways of drifting cloud shadows, and who had for speech the scream of untamed devils. Though he had watched and watched by many a trail and sown the district with traps and poison, it had so far netted him nothing. Unless one counted the glimpse he had once gotten, or thought he had gotten, of one of the big cats one dusk—a dim half-guessed shadow in the fickle light. It had been behind him as he made his way through some dense timber, and the vision had been accompanied by a queer sensation along his spine that made his blond hair stand up.

Dave Baxter was becoming increasingly piqued by the situation. This pair of outlaws on whose trail he was camped were rapidly depopulating the preserve of all wildlife save that of the predatory persuasion. Despite his presence in the vicinity, the killing was continuing and the best of his craft had been mocked by the cougars. Daily he had come upon the carcasses of deer or elk that had been recently done to death and left lying with but a small portion eaten.

He knew there were two of the marauders; often he had been aware of them nearby, had felt them, heard the warning sounds of birds and squirrels at their passing. The trails were full of history, for stalking with these beasts was more than a word, it was a finished science. As each day brought fresh evidence of the boldness and cunning of the outlaws a disgust for himself and his woodcraft settled upon Baxter.

The cougars' original panic had abated. They had learned that the man, though undoubtedly on their trail, was easy to evade, and a malign curiosity had taken the place of their initial fear. Several times they had studied the ranger from some unguessed vantage, and they had watched his camp at night when a bright fire lighted the small pyramid of his khaki tent.

So the days drew out into three full weeks with still no vantage on the part of the ranger. Winter would soon close in on the high country. Dave had about decided to go down and gather a dog pack, when the chance he had awaited so long took him almost unprepared.

He was sitting one afternoon on a slope overlooking a deep valley, pipe in mouth. In the morning, he decided, he would go down for the dogs, for he had acknowledged himself defeated to date. Suddenly his pipe dropped from his mouth. A faint sound downslope had snapped his senses to full alertness. Abruptly the biggest cougar he had ever seen slipped shadowlike across a cleared space forty yards below. Quick as light itself the rifle had leaped to Dave's shoulder, but just too late. Just as he lowered it, a second cougar, a trifle smaller, showed momentarily. Dave's aim and the report were simultaneous. He saw the cat give a great loose leap and he knew he had scored. With a thrill of exultation he plunged downslope.

From that hour on the affair became a swift grim war between the ranger and the big male cat which was left: the one, superperfect master of woodcraft and slaying; the other, whose claw and fang were trap and rifle, at least equally vigilant. It was a duel such as neither contestant had ever fought before. Every move that either made by day or night became a vital part of the game.

The big male was no ordinary cougar, as Dave was to learn. With the death of his mate his craft and audacity seemed tripled. Half his caution had been for her at any rate—the third mate he had seen killed in his long war with man and civilization. The span of life that remained to him would be one unrelenting battle, he knew, but a desperate ferocity had taken the place of fear within him.

At first he had thought of putting the region far behind him, but that uncertainty was too great. The deer forests he loved were scarce, and the world was full of enemies for such as he. True, the danger here was great, but the rich feeding on elk meat tempted him beyond all caution. From the first the elk bands had worked a threefold fascination on him, primarily because they were a new kind of game; also because of their unprecedented size. There was a sense of power in triumphing over these tall beasts; likewise their meat was stronger, richer than any venison.

So his killings continued and the manner of them was, if anything, more audacious than before. But now he never killed twice in the same vicinity, and never returned to a kill to feed. Nor did he follow any of the old game trails.

Dave Baxter came of a stubborn breed; also his pride was piqued. He packed a skin-lined tent upcountry, determined to have the slayer's pelt at any cost. Yet with all his dogged persistence it was not booked for Dave himself to bring the outlaw low.

One afternoon after the second snow the cougar was reclining in one of his favorite resting places deep in the gnarled embrace of an ancient spruce whose matted branches overlapped. This was one of several such lookouts which he chose according to the breeze. Screened from above and on two sides, he could look out across the deep, narrow valley to the peaks across the way, and down a series of rocky ramps to the stream bed far below. The mountain slope beneath him acted as a sounding board, warning him of any stir of life for hundreds of yards around.

Afar a coyote sounded his first faint rally call, cue for all night prowlers to bestir themselves. The cougar dropped from his branch with a silent rubbery undulation and melted like a spook into the gathering shadows. Thereafter there was neither sign nor sound to betray him until, sometime later, a long low shadow emerged from the denser shadows in the bottom of the valley. This was but a few hundred yards upwind from where a band of elk bunched together for the night. From here on the cougar inched forward soundlessly until, with a chain-lightning rush, he was upon the back of a sleek cow. He felled her by his usual method, breaking her neck.

Always at this point had come a scattering and panic flight of the elk. Instead there was a blasting and bugling from several bulls and a milling and bunching of their number, much as buffalo might have bunched together when wolves came out of the night. This was because the yard in which the herd had clustered was flanked on one side by high rock cliffs and on the other by dense low timber. The cougar's attack had come along their one avenue of escape. Cornered, the leading bulls had elected to turn upon the killer, and the entire band followed suit, closing in upon the enemy.

Panicked, the cougar leaped upon the crowding backs, trying to claw his way over them to escape, but the sweeping antlers of a wrathful bull hooked him off and he was down again among the trampling hoofs. The slashing fore-hoof of a bull flattened him to earth with a staved rib. Wauling with pain he crawled his way up and over the milling backs as before, fighting his way wildly toward the open, as he thought. Somehow he actually did gain the edge of the herd, on the cliffside. He sprang high but could not scale the nearly perpendicular face of the rock. The cougar slithered back, claws spread, to fall fighting into the tossing antlers. The inflamed elk, acting as one, closed in upon him.

Though the cougar fought insanely in those last moments it was useless, for the herd spirit had turned upon him. This was the terrible fury of the hunted bent upon annihilating a wanton slayer. The elk pinned him in a recess between the cliffside and a boulder mass that was choked with windfalls. And when they were done an old and weathered bull lifted on his antlers the limp thing that was left and tossed it wrathfully into the thickets.

It was there that the crows and buzzards discovered it next morning, and so led Dave Baxter to the hidden spot.

▪ The Devil of the Woods

FOR A LONG TIME LABAN SMALL STOOD IN THE EARLY MORN-
ing light, looking at those splayed, handlike tracks in the
new snow, each print coming to a peak of fierce claw marks.
The tracks disappeared a hundred feet away in the blue-
black shadows of the spruce. Before him a marten, caught
the night before in one of his trap sets, had been partially
devoured, its prime pelt torn to ribbons. This was the fourth
pelt destroyed on Laban's trap line in the past few nights.
At first he had thought foxes were robbing his traps.

His small, sharp eyes glittered like black glass. But the
dark somber spruce and the shadows beneath them gave
back nothing; the winter stillness was complete.

Laban rearranged his set and moved on along his line.
Martens he killed in small traps or deadfalls; fox, muskrat
and beaver he caught in steel traps; lynx and otter he
strangled in wire snares; and the tiny snow-white stoat and
ermine he caught by their small pink tongues on heavy
strips of iron smeared with bacon grease and laid out in the
freezing air.

For twenty-five years Laban Small had lived in the wilderness.

As he moved between the endless rows of tree trunks he

felt that malignant eyes were watching him. Again and again he stopped to peer back along his trail.

A gray fox had been caught in the next set, and like the marten, the carcass had been partially eaten, torn and mutilated till the pelt was worthless. Another trap in the brush had been sprung and carried away. The trail showed where the robber had dragged trap and clog into a deep ravine and buried it in the snow.

"Couldn't even leave me the trap, ye thievin' devil!" Laban's thin, harsh voice broke out. "Two hundred dollars in fur ye chewed up an' done me out of already." Cursing, he backed out of the narrow gulley.

As he went on along the trap line his spare, aging body was imbued with the strength of rage. He was pulling all his traps now and carrying them slung over his shoulder. The enemy he was pitted against destroyed all hope of a fur catch.

He found three more prime pelts torn and ruined by the trap robber. Of the twenty-odd traps Laban visited, only three had been unmolested. By midafternoon he was at the farthest limit of his range. He was descending a steep hogback through a stand of fir. The winter sunshine was breaking through the clouds when Laban stopped suddenly, dropping his load in the snow. Abruptly he plunged back up the slope and crouched behind a tree at the crest of the hogback.

From beneath the drooping boughs of the spruce wood he had just quitted, a humped, dark shape took form; a ragged, sooty black and brown beast that lumbered like a small bear, lighter colored along its back and darker underneath, in direct contradiction to all other forest creatures. For a space it paused, its sinister green-shadowed eyes fixing those of the man peering round the tree trunk sixty feet away. Then the creature did a strange thing. Shading its eyes with an almost human gesture from the sunlight, it looked long at the man from under its heavy black paw. A shiver ran through the body of Laban Small and he rose with a panic shout.

"Overlook me, will ye—Black Devil!" he cried and rushed at the beast with his light belt ax in his hand, for he carried no rifle on his trap rounds. The animal melted back into the shadows of the spruce and disappeared.

For minutes Laban stood in the dusky shadows of the trees, fighting down the *habitant's* superstitious dread of this vile and uncanny beast, which was known to trappers as Glutton, carcajou, Woods Devil, and to the Indians as Bad Dog, the red man's ultimate term of loathing. The carcajou, he knew, had a cunning surpassing that of the craftiest fox, to which was added a diabolical passion to destroy and to defile. Worst of all, trappers believed that evil fortune fastened upon one who had been "overlooked" by a wolverine.

Laban's first thought was to leave this valley at once. But it was so rich in fur! And he had his trapper's pride. To go in to the settlement and admit that he had been driven out of his range by a carcajou would be too humiliating.

"Ye won't run me out of my range, ye skulkin' devil!" he cried to the shadows. "Me an' you'll fight this thing out an' see who's who in these woods!"

It was past dark when Laban, weighted down with sixty pounds of traps, completed his twelve-mile rounds and arrived at his cabin. He dropped his clanking load in a corner.

"Our luck's gone!" he said in a high snarl to his Indian wife. "We been robbed. The devil himself's found us out. Injun Devil! No wonder I ain't slept for two nights."

Quick fear was in the woman's sloe eyes: "Thief she Injun Devil? You make sure?"

"Tracked him, one end of the line to t'other!" Laban did not want to tell her he had been "overlooked" by the beast. That possible evil spell he must keep to himself. He bolted some food by the fire and then said to his woman, "Boil up lye an' water. We got work to do."

He was planning. "The varmint's old an' wise. I'll keep on settin' bait fer a spell, then plant double sets, one with bait an' one without. That ought to fetch him."

In the fur country it was considered next to impossible to trap a wolverine, for the little beast could smell iron through three feet of snow, and detect man smell like no other creature of the forest. Yet unless he could kill the animal, Laban's take of pelts for the winter would be practically nothing.

While the tub of lye and water was heating, Laban placed his traps one by one in the open fire. Then he laid each trap in the boiling lye to further destroy all human scent. He would henceforth handle the traps with gloves which had likewise been treated with lye.

"It's the devil of the woods himself I got to outsmart!" he said.

Again that night Laban slept poorly. He dreamed that the eyes of the animal fiend were watching him through the cabin walls.

For a week thereafter a battle of wits between Laban and the robber was waged, with the vantage mounting in favor of the wolverine. The woods devil was ahead of him on every trail. Laban carried his rifle each day, but not a glimpse did he catch of his enemy.

Ordinarily in winter scarce a score of words a week would pass between Laban and his wife. Now he talked by the hour about his death hunt, and the woman saw fear in his eyes. She said nothing but Laban knew that she knew he had been "overlooked" by the wolverine. Her primitive superstition was added to his own weight of dread.

Laban had planted double and triple sets with his lye-treated traps, but the wolverine was not fooled. In some dense brush Laban set up a cocked rifle, and fixed in front of its muzzle a dead grouse, attached to a cord fastened to the trigger. Around the gun he had piled more brush and logs so that the wolverine would have to approach the bait from in front.

At another spot, over a little bubbling spring that was open all winter, he hung a dead partridge on a smoked string. Beneath the partridge he concealed a wolf trap in the shallow water, covering the pan with a dab of green moss so that it looked like a stone just showing above the surface. Any creature drawn by the scent of the bird would step out on the counterfeit stone to examine the bait more closely.

But the following day Laban found his craft was matched and mocked—and worse. The wolverine had forced his way through the massed brush and, coming up behind the gun, had chewed the cord in two and carried off the grouse.

When he came to the spring set a cry of agony was wrung from the old trapper. The steel jaws beneath the moss had been sprung. Scattered about the spring were tufts of fluffy black fur with long silver-white guard hairs. It was not the wolverine he had caught. It *had* been a prime silver fox in the trap, the greatest prize known to trappers, worth more than all his other pelts combined. And the woods devil had found and destroyed it.

That day Laban gave over all idea of garnering furs. At the end of his trap line, six miles from his cabin, he built a cache where next day he stored blankets, some bacon, corn meal, beans and tobacco, so that at any time he could make a night camp there. He cut and piled over his cache a crisscrossed mass of logs. Over these he poured water from a nearby stream, which quickly froze, locking the mass into a fortress which it would have taken a man with an ax an hour to break into.

For some days he had no cause to use the cache; then one afternoon, seeing recent tracks of the woods devil, he decided to camp at the cache and take up the trail at dawn. But the cache no longer existed. With a patience and strength that seemed not of earth, the carcajou had gnawed and clawed away the ice and wrenched apart the heaped tree trunks. The bacon he had devoured, the beans and meal he had scattered and fouled. Almost all the traps were missing and as a final touch of deviltry, Laban's very tobacco was gone. The tracks in the snow were fresh. Had Laban happened along an hour earlier he might have surprised the robber.

Beside the trail was a brown liquid stain in the snow and a small chunk of tobacco. Laban followed on. Other dribbles of brown were tobacco juice beyond a doubt. Into the woodsman's mind sprang a strange hope. Possibly the sweetish molasses flavor of the tobacco had appealed to the robber as a special delicacy. No organism would be proof against the sickness that would follow if the creature had swallowed the stuff. The tracks in the snow wavered and zigzagged drunkenly.

Within a hundred yards he saw where the carcajou had paused to vomit. The tobacco was doing its work! A few hundred yards more and Laban saw movement in a dense blowdown. The wolverine suddenly emerged from the down timber and went reeling and lurching away between the trees. As the man fired, the beast pitched forward, struggled up and sank again.

From the snow the green-shadowed eyes of the wolverine glared at Laban as he rushed up. A harsh churring snarl filled the air. As he looked down at that blunt, formidable head the man saw what a lifetime in the forest had not yet shown him—a creature with no fiber of fear in all its being, and the sight enraged him.

With a rabid cry Laban was upon the beast, swinging his belt ax. But the ax was arrested before it fell. This devil of the woods had made him suffer for weeks. It had robbed him of his hard-won catch. The idea came to Laban to take the creature alive and make it suffer in turn. He beat the animal insensible with the flat of his ax and then bound its legs together with strips of babiche thong which he always carried with him. He muzzled the grim jaws also with thongs. When the animal stirred again Laban kicked its solid ribs till they resounded.

"Black Devil! Overlook me, will you? Who is master now?"

Ferociously he stamped and capered round the hated beast. He tried to cow and terrify it. He cut the air over its head with the ax so close the blade grazed its skull. He chopped down into the hard-packed snow so close that the ax edge scraped its muzzle. But the creature would not flinch. The small greenish eyes still fixed implacably on the man despite its nausea. Laban had to start back.

He cut pine saplings for a travois on which to drag the animal on the long trek back. Fierce elation filled his scrawny frame with energy. It was long after dark when his small figure came up the trail to the cabin. His wife cried out at sight of the animal.

"What do you think of Laban Small now as a trapper, woman?" he shouted. "Wait till they hear of this down at the settlement! How I tracked this devil for three weeks and pinched his toes at the last! And they'll have the story, come Christmas! We go in to the settlement for the holiday this year, woman, and take this devil with us—alive!"

He had arrived at this decision on the long trail home.

The continuous low growling of the wolverine filled the cabin like the sound of a saw.

"Watch him," ordered Laban, "while I make a place for him in the shed. If he gets loose, shoot him."

He returned presently and dragged the wolverine out to the strong log hut where he stored his furs. He had stapled two lengths of trap chain to the log walls on each side. The other ends he padlocked tightly about the neck of the animal. He kicked it again, cut the thongs with his knife and laughed jeeringly as the wolverine raged, but was held in the middle of the floor unable to reach him.

Laban ate scarcely anything that night in his excitement. He talked long by the fire. He would make the wolverine suffer for a time. After showing it alive in the town he would devise for it the sort of death it deserved. He scarcely slept for thinking of his captive. He lay concocting the tale he would tell in the settlement. He would never even mention the tobacco. How the liquor would flow in his honor! It was less than two weeks until Christmas.

Next day he had meant to reset his traps, but he spent only two hours on his line and was back by midday. He had to see his captive again, to make sure that it suffered enough —but not to the death. And to see if there was yet a sign of fear in the animal.

There was none. The wolverine, in fact, was doing quite well. Its wounds were beginning to heal and it seemed impervious to the cold. Its breath rose in a steam in the icy air; its heavy bearlike body seemed able to generate heat and temper its frosty prison.

In the cabin the woman had set a pan of meat scraps aside. Laban flew into a rage.

"What are you doin', woman? Makin' a pet of that devil?"

She shrank back, but he knew with a chill what she was doing. She was trying to conciliate the demon. But Laban raged on.

"Near five thousand dollars that devil owes me. But wait. Come Christmas and he'll pay me well——"

He threw the carcajou a small handful of meat and fat. Just enough to keep it alive until he had achieved his vengeance. Just beyond the captive's reach he set a full pan of meat, to torture it.

Again the following day he spent but a couple of hours on his trap line. He was thinking continually of the wolverine. The next day and the next, he hurried home to make sure his prisoner was secure and that it was suffering.

But the wolverine seemed doing well in spite of everything. Its spirit was in no way broken. It could move but a foot and a half, but it was doing what it would have done in the wild to recover from its hurts, spending most of its time lying on its side, wetting its paw with healing saliva and rubbing it over its wounds, which were healing rapidly.

Again and again Laban stirred it up by prodding it fiercely with a pole. He listened with delight to its savage growling, watching it score deep marks in the wood with its powerful teeth.

By the end of a week all the traps on Laban's line were reset and he was beginning to collect pelts again. But the furs gave him little pleasure. What was consuming him was the fact that he had taken a woods devil alive—but no one had heard of it.

Early the second week he decided he could wait no longer for his trip to the settlement. His wife begged him not to try to make the trip alone with the wolverine. He watched and caught her trying to turn the animal loose. The superstitious half-Indian woman was in mortal dread of the beast's powers. For that Laban cursed her and refused to allow her to go to the settlement with him. Once more he clubbed the wolverine into insensibility and lashed it to his sledge.

He started alone at midforenoon, his rifle slung by a strap over his shoulder. For several hours he made fair headway until he came to the steep descent at the mouth of the valley, where the winds kept the snow crusted and glassy. Carefully he worked down the slope, pausing often to cut footholds with his belt ax, easing the sledge down with the line. He had the descent almost whipped when a foot went out from under him. The loaded sledge got away and the line tripped and threw him flat. Sledge, ax and rifle went skidding down a hundred yard slope and out of sight among the trees. Laban himself slithered downward until he caught the trunk of a dead pine. His rifle was sticking out of a snowdrift far below. His ax had disappeared. And the wolverine! What had become of it?

The sledge had shot over a notch of snow between drifts and dropped out of sight below.

Laban let go and slid down to his rifle, then scrambled to a spot from which he could see below. The sledge had plunged over a ten-foot drop and struck an outcropping rock, splitting itself in two. The split had broken the thongs that held the wolverine's forelegs. The animal was upreared, struggling to free its hindquarters.

Laban knelt for a steady aim. He didn't take time to think that when it speared into the drift, the rifle barrel would be packed with soft snow. He never knew what hit him when the weapon exploded in his face. He was dead before his body fell back.

The abominable sound of the explosion above him goaded the wolverine to renewed effort. A few more tremendous heaves got him out of the already loosened thongs that held his hind legs.

He squatted then in the snow, shading his eyes with a blunt paw, and looked upward to where the man lay. There was nothing evil nor threatening in the gesture, except to the minds of the ignorant. There was simply a glare of sun on the snow and the wolverine had wit enough to shade his eyes.

Neither was there anything of a dread or evil in the beast himself. Men called him Devil because he could outwit them. He was simply a superclever beast with a brain that in some ways rivaled man's, for he was one of the oldest living forms left on the planet. Five hundred thousand years ago, before the First Ice Age, the wolverine, as he is now, had met the cave lion and the saber-toothed tiger, and bested them in craft. Through the ages he had developed his wile, courage, and will to survive.

The petty persecution of Laban Small had left little or no impression upon his imperturbable confidence. Now the man lay still with a stillness the wolverine knew well. Calm with the immutable calm of the great, hurrying for nothing, he moved away into the silent woods.

▪ The Secret Place

For the second time that day the trumpeting of elephants came echoing from far over the jungled valleys to disturb El Robo in his mud bath. El Robo knew the meaning of those sounds. They told of a ceremony, a ritual in honor of a monarch, a newly ascended monarch and doubtless a young one, and they rankled El Robo to the depths of his cantankerous nature.

El Robo was an outlaw, and a criminal. There were, as is often the case in the human kingdom, extenuating circumstances. In his young prime the prolonged pain of a broken tusk had soured his nature, a tusk being no more nor less than an oversized tooth, with an oversized ache in proportion. A toothache lasting two or three years can ruin any disposition and it had rendered El Robo unfit for the life of the herd. The wise old leaders, doubtless able to predict even then the bane of the young bull's future, had finally been obliged to cast him out. That was forty years ago and not one of those years had gone to sweeten the old rogue's nature.

Still, life had not all been harsh and lean. There was satisfaction of a sort in simply being a chronic crank, with undisputed feeding grounds, private mud baths, neither law nor family to curtail one's wandering, and unlimited time to humor one's whims. Besides, El Robo relished the silence, the sense of aloneness and the constant watchfulness and dangerous exploration that composed his life. Sometimes he dreamed of the other kind of life, of companionship, a mate of his own, and the security of numbers. Once in his early prime he had wanted this enough to do battle for it. He had pitted himself against the two leading bulls of a small herd and taken it over. But group life entailed responsibilities and disciplines which he found irksome, and finally intolerable. And so upon a night of scented breeze and calling moonlight he simply wandered away and did not return.

In time, having broken all elephant laws, he had become feared and hated by his own kind. Battle-scarred, a broken-tusked veteran of sixty, he had but to show himself to a herd to call down all the challenge and anathema the elephant tongue possessed. His temper had become that of a peevish rhino. He would go along the jungle trails rumbling and blasting challenges which law-abiding herd bulls had long since come to disregard. He would wait days in a certain bath, hoping some other bull would come and try to claim it. Finally in sheer frustration he would climb out and tear up a stand of young trees. He hated man, too.

This that had aroused El Robo today was the salute to a victor, whose prowess the herd was acclaiming. It stirred all the old resentment in him. Up out of his bath he heaved, a gaunt almost prehistoric African beast, nearly twelve feet tall at the shoulder, red-eyed with a sudden upsurge of fury. His trunk curled upward, his blaring challenge ending in a berserk squeal.

He stood then, great fan ears awave, hoping for an answer, yet fearing the usual insult of silence. Unexpectedly from over the hills, came a trumpet in reply. Blasting his surprise, El Robo surged up the bank. An ignorant young bull, doubtless one who had not yet learned to ignore the challenges of the renegade.

Some years had passed since El Robo had clashed with any sort of adversary, and all the pent-up violence of his nature called for an outlet. A fine running horse would have been put to it to keep up with him for sheer speed, even though El Robo had the handicap of dense thickets in his path and young trees, many of which he snapped off at their bases as he passed. Because of the wonderful conformity of his muscles, his great feet plied with a catlike surety and the ground shook beneath him.

The herd was drawn up waiting when El Robo arrived. All feeding had ceased and a fighting ring was already forming, for there were set laws and niceties in such affairs and every elephant knew what must come. The newly acclaimed leader, a tall rangy bull of some thirty years, stood well to the fore. Behind him were three other herd bulls and several leading cows.

El Robo's advance slowed to a walk, but he stamped belligerently into the waiting circle, raising his trunk to renew his defiance. Before he could sound forth again the young leader had repeated the challenge himself with a dignified assurance that enraged the old rogue afresh. He precipitated the combat with an abrupt charge from the side. A less mighty opponent would have been flung off balance or overthrown, but the young bull took up the shock with agile legwork that brought him head-on with his attacker.

Trunk curled under, skull lowered, tusks swung down, he met and stopped the other's rush, ungiving as the rock face of a mountain. In the prolonged head-to-head trial of strength that followed, there was no sound but the blasting breaths of the fighters, the occasional dry scrape of hide on hide, and the restless stamping of the watching bulls, a kind of rhythmic pummeling of the earth. Straining head to head, each with six tons' pressure behind him, straining until there seemed no possibility of giving on either side, until skulls cracked. They were titans evenly matched, the one with youth and resilience on his side, his long legs as symmetrical as the smooth trunks of the jungle gum trees; the other with an even greater bulk and weight and the wile of age behind him.

It was this wile which made El Robo abruptly cease his steamroller pushing and utilize the other's overbalanced weight to spit him back of the shoulder with his one good tusk. The maneuver was effective but the tusk met bone, and the young bull, pivoting swiftly, caught El Robo full in the side, all but overthrowing him. Driving the rogue before him with heaving ripping tusks, the leader forced the fight through the cordon of watchers, and the bulls of his herd trumpeted with excitement.

Not until he was back among the trees did El Robo regain an equal footing with his opponent. Handicapped as he was, he had, through the years, developed great skill with his single tusk, a skill which had more than once undone a foe. Now he utilized the trees to cover his tuskless side and fenced cleverly with the other, side-stepping all head-on rushes. He knew by now that no rush of his would overthrow the other, nor could he win by endurance, for the younger bull had far more of that than he. El Robo was outclassed and he knew it, but he could not bring himself to back away with lowered trunk in token of defeat.

Holding the other off with crafty side thrusts, he waited for a strategic moment and left his right shoulder purposely unguarded. The young bull came in with a rush, but El

Robo wasn't there. Before the enemy could wheel, he gathered himself again, and the single yellow tusk drove into the other's side. Blood ran down the leader's foreleg, but his scream was more rage than pain. He wheeled and came in with the shock of a catapult. Thud and scrape of huge bodies coming together, a rumble of pain, and the old rogue was down, blood dripping from his mouth from some deep internal wound.

Even before El Robo's grudging signal of defeat, all saw that the battle was over. Slowly now, the young leader backed away and his attacker was permitted to rise. With head low and in great pain, El Robo backed out of the circle and into the dense, surrounding thickets, leaving the young hero to trumpet victory for the second time that day. It was followed by the herd's answering salute.

El Robo moved away with ponderous slowness, for his injuries were many and deep. Sometime later, standing in a dense wet glen, it came to him that his wounds were fatal. That meant that he had a final journey to make. Where, or how far he did not know, but something in him knew, and that something drew him irresistibly southward. He had only to follow that inner urge as best he could.

From his camp a mile downriver, Colin McArthur, field scout for the British Ivory Syndicate, listened with interest to the far wild trumpetings of the elephant herd. As it happened, he had been following this particular herd for more than a week from the northern edge of the Rift valleys into the jungle country of Tanganyika. From years of experience with the African elephant he read in the sounds something of special moment.

Perhaps no living white man knew more of the ways of these giants than Colin McArthur, for in his peculiar calling he derived all the thrill that an artist knows in the pursuit of his task. Also by some chemistry of blood he seemed immune to African diseases and climatic downpulls. Watching, studying the signs of the elephant trails with his two black carriers, McArthur was not elephant hunting in the usual sense; something of far greater import drew him on. In this last field trip he had had strange new intimations of the elephant arcanum, and a certain hope, long held, had been rekindled. This had to do with a theory of many African hunters—based on the fact that there was so little elephant fossil to be found even in elephant country—that there *was* such a thing as an elephant burial ground, a final sanctuary sought by the great beasts at the time of death.

By the time the second victorious trumpeting sounded, McArthur had moved in close enough to the scene of combat to witness its end through his binoculars. His glass picked out the defeated one, a mighty old bull, as he had surmised from the sound of his challenges, now badly wounded. The bull, he saw, had but a single tusk. McArthur watched the old one move slowly off into the forest. Ordering his two askaris to follow him at a considerable distance, he set off at once on the elephant's trail.

The trail led him straight south, and it was marked by bloody signs which increased rather than diminished. The Englishman noted other things as the hours passed: that the great bull stopped neither to eat nor drink and that he traveled with a total disregard of existing trails, or of caution, facts which quickened the hunter's pulses as he went. For if the animal was mortally wounded it was just possible that the thing for which he had waited for years was about to transpire.

In time the trail led out of the jungle into the desolate almost treeless land of the Rift valleys. This was a wilderness of red earth and lava rock formation with isolate crater-topped mountains. McArthur halted for the night in a spot of sparse vegetation where the few trees grew gnarled and twisted from the battle for roothold in the rocky soil. His carriers caught up with him by nightfall.

At dawn McArthur took up the lone trail once more. Toward midmorning he came upon a small streamlet that flowed out of the mountainside, doubtless from some lake in the crater above. The water tasted faintly sulphurous. The tracks of the wounded bull led upward now, around the shoulder of the mountain. McArthur climbed until the nest of wild valleys below could be seen to radiate from the mountain's base. At least two of these appeared blocked by lava deposit.

There were many elephant signs now, including what seemed a definite trail and marks where the great beasts had scraped against the rock walls in passing. Rounding a turn in the trail McArthur found himself standing a hundred yards above yet another valley, one broader and greener than the rest and strewn with rocks and boulders of a whitish cast. He descended with a mounting sense of excitement in his breast, somehow certain that here was one of those rare spots of earth where no man—no white man at least—had ever been. A secret place of the wild, it was. A place of death, he now began to know, for what he had taken for a jumbled mass of rock appeared suddenly as a field of whitened bones. Elephant fossil—most of it ancient and huger than any McArthur had ever seen. It lay scattered along the valley floor as far as he could see, many of the skeletons honeycombed by time.

So he had come upon it at last, the living legend, and the answer to every ivory hunter's dream: an elephant cemetery where a thousand generations of elephants must have come to die. Everywhere about him, free as light or air, was treasure, ivory for the taking. And all of it, for the moment, at least, belonged to him.

McArthur moved on down the valley, poking and peering, climbing through and over mounds of fossil, examining the great tusks, dark with age but all in perfect preservation, as is the nature of ivory. Weird—and no end to it. Picking his way among mighty leg bones, traversing long arcades of arching ribs; he saw whitened skulls as large as boulders.

He was in a state of wonder, aimlessly exploring, when from behind him came sudden warning. A shadow crossed the sun and in his ears was a blaring trumpet call.

What McArthur saw in that instant was a gray and hairy mountain of elephant flesh bearing down upon him with eyes that were red wicks of violence. It was the vanquished one-tusked bull whose trail he had followed here.

Hours before, El Robo had reached the sanctuary, knowing it because the urge that had driven him abruptly ceased. He found the spot that seemed to be his own and lay down. Like a fallen tree of the forest or any other natural thing, he lay waiting for the sun and air and earth to take him back. In this there was a lonely majesty such as man himself rarely attains.

The peace of the end was already upon him when the human interloper, prowling among the bones, roused him to righteous fury and brought him heaving to his feet. All his life El Robo had defied elephant law, but this final duty, to defend the sanctuary, could not be denied. He could not die with this violator at large in the ancestral resting place of his kind. El Robo lumbered forward at a painful trot.

McArthur dove through a cage of giant ribs and up over a boulder to a ledge of rock where he could turn and send a

rifle ball into the charging bull. Though he could scarcely
have missed hitting the beast, to all appearances the shot
had no effect whatever. There was another blast that shook
the canyon air and the elephant came on, blanket ears flapping, tail out stiff with wrath. That gray looping trunk
would surely reach his ledge. McArthur scrambled frantically over rocks and thence to the ground and ran for his
life down the valley. His one hope was that his pursuer
was a sick and dying beast and that any instant might bring
on his complete collapse.

But the monster gave him not an instant's pause for a second try with his rifle. Through a pile of broken fossil he
plunged, the jagged points and edges clutching at his clothes.
His canteen caught by its strap and he left it dangling.
The small pack on his shoulders he unstrapped and
shrugged out of as he ran. A moment later he tripped and
fell flat, his rifle slipping from sight in the rubble beneath.
No time to retrieve it. His horror now was of being caught
in some cul-de-sac among the bones, which were no handicap at all to his pursuer. In fact the sound of the bull's
coming on was of bones crackling, shattering with every
step.

Ahead of him McArthur spied a cranny in the cliffside.
If only it were deep enough! He had to chance it. He made
the fissure in the rock by the narrowest of margins. Behind
him there was a rush like a wind squall and the elephant's
bulk darkened the opening. The hole was not as deep as he
had hoped. Desperately McArthur squirmed into the farthest cranny. The gray trunk came in after him, feeling along
the walls of the cave and blasting fetid air. The bull could
do better than this, McArthur knew, for the fissure was
wide enough for at least part of the great head. Beyond this
the bull might gouge away the rocky sides. . . .

McArthur crouched and waited, gripped by a fear that was like the numbness of catalepsy. The great head was pressing now, the searching trunk all but touched him. When the head drew back it was, he knew, for the purpose of widening the opening.

In these terrible moments McArthur had forgotten that his inexorable pursuer was a dying beast. Now he saw, at very close range, that the great bull was virtually dead, yet animated and driven on by some ingrained code of the elephant kind. And suddenly the man understood. Always in McArthur's mind the elephant had stood as the hierophant of the animal world, whose laws deserved man's respect. This bull now was answering an urge that was literally stronger than death, and certainly not without nobility, to keep inviolate this final resting place sacred to his race.

With realization came sympathy. In his heart the Englishman made solemn pact with Almighty God and the elephant kind: if he came through this thing alive he would keep the secret of this place, betray it never.

As if the old bull had sensed the unspoken promise he halted his assault upon the rocky entrance and backed a few paces with trunk turned under and massive head strangely anod. Then he knelt, slowly and carefully easing his six-ton bulk to earth. It was the end, McArthur knew, for soon utter and complete silence settled over the valley of the dead.

▪ The Odyssey of Old Specs

It was mid-march, too early by a matter of weeks to be abroad, and the young raccoon was most unhappy, lean, cold, and brittle of fur. Not another coon was stirring throughout the entire length of Big Tamarack swamp. He knew; he had wandered half the day, and a thankless business it was in a birdless, frogless world.

He sat on a log surveying the immemorial silence and loneliness of the swamp woods. Like all his kind, and his kind are all bandits after their fashion, he was masked with a band of black circling each bright, canny eye and running back to the ears. But the young coon's mask was a good shade blacker than usual, with a distinct bar crossing the nose like a pair of huge spectacles, setting off the silvery fur above and below. It was this that later gave him the name by which he was known in the region.

Young Specs didn't know what had got him out of his hollow tree so early, but he did know that he was strangely metamorphosed. He had gone to sleep a little over three months before as a mere stripling, and had slept himself, so to speak, into man's estate. Like a good many of us who are not coons, that transformation was not a little disquieting. He had grown a good inch overall, while he slept. Even his feet had grown and he had taken on girth; his delicate cat-like whiskers were longer and more luxuriant and his chief pride, his black-and-white-ringed tail, had become a very plume of vanity. He had even achieved something in the way of long pants, the thick fur on his short legs having developed into heavy chaps that reached almost to his black feet. Result: he was in love, in love with a raccoonness he had never even seen.

It was a strange and wonderful sensation. It made him feel, in spite of his loneliness, that the world was his oyster, though how to open the thing was a mystery. Natural knowledge, however, that evanescent sixth sense that flickers on in the wiser among us when the other five are at fault, told him what to do about it. He trekked.

It was not until the fourth day, however, that he encountered another coon, a grizzled old bandit, abroad early out of sheer cantankerousness. Young Specs hurried forward eagerly. He wanted to join up with the old fellow, but the other warned him off with a long, hard look and a growl. Specs growled too, and the sound of it left him with another bit of self-knowledge. Even his voice had changed.

Specs felt his youth terribly. He was not to be spurned, however. Here was one of his own kind, not the answer to his dreams, yet grunt, growl and whisker an exact copy of himself. He fell in behind, content to dog the other's footsteps, sensing the promise of adventure, romance and full, crowding life in store.

He was right. The old one was the goods; an experienced coon-about-swamp, and no better mentor could have been found. He covered the swamp in great five-mile circles, and in four hours Young Specs learned more than the whole first year of life had taught him. He had foolishly believed the winter woods were devoid of food. But the old coon knew a dozen handy wrinkles. He visited every dead or hollow tree in the swamp, prying into all their crannies for grubs. Into a hole in one of these he rammed an arm to the shoulder and rifled a squirrel's nest of its sleepy half-grown young.

On the edge of the swamp he tarried a long time on a rush-grown bank that was literally honeycombed with wood-mouse runways. Here a fellow had only to sit and wait until dinner ran into his paws, course by course. Young Specs followed suit, squatting to do a bit of mousing on his own, about a dozen feet away. In his absorption he failed to keep a weather eye out and the old coon was suddenly on him tooth and claw, before he had even time to throw himself on his back in the defensive stance of his kind. He was bitten and mauled and driven whining into the thickets, but he circled back, undampened, to follow on until night.

Next day he was hanging about waiting when the old one appeared. He followed again at a safe distance and that day his education reached its height. The old boar, it appeared, was no very nice character and Young Specs was initiated into the ways of the real freebooter. Toward dusk the old one stole by circuitous ways to a lonely backwoods farm. Time and again he turned and threatened the youngster with mayhem and worse if he did not turn back, but Specs could not have even if he would. He had been born to take part in just such reckless forays as this; it was his heritage and he knew it with every drop of blood within him. He knew the danger that threatened, yet he followed even closer as the old bandit slipped beneath the rail fence. He heard subdued squawks from a henhouse somewhat later and then the roar of a dog, and it was as if he had done this thing by himself a dozen times before.

He was waiting when the boar rushed desperately into

the woods with a plump hen dangling from his jaws, and he fell in alongside, eager to fight it out with the other as long as allowed. The dog luckily had been chained, but very shortly they were apprised that he was loose. No stream in which to lose their trails, and snow would not do. So they fled, backs humping like measuring worms, thick fur rolling, time too pressing even for the old one to snarl at Young Specs' presence.

The dog's yapping bluster gave him away as a tyro. He was dangerous all the same, coming fast, with the farmer probably behind him. The old coon waited till the last minute before stuffing his kill in a hole beneath a tree root. Specs thought they were taking to the trees for safety as he followed up the trunk of an ancient oak, but the boar halted on the lowest branch for the dog to come up.

Without hesitation he launched himself at the back of the mongrel as he came beneath the tree. He struck true, gripping with all four claws and the dog howled with fright at the suddenness of the thing. Specs launched himself downward, too, his belly thumping the hard ground for his pains.

An experienced coon can be a terrible fighting machine. The dog was twice the size of the coon, yet in strategy the coon was his master at every turn. No animal in the world can take so much punishment with apparently so little pain as a coon. Each time the mongrel appeared to get a killing grip, the coon slipped the hold by turning within his heavy loose hide.

Back and forth they threshed among the bushes, Young Specs dancing about them in a frenzy. They broke apart and Specs flung himself into the breach, eager to do all a youngster could to help the old highwayman. He got in one bite and was seized by the neck and shaken like a muff. The old one saved him from being shredded to bits.

The farmer had not followed the dog and within a few minutes the mongrel had had more than enough. With a dozen bites in his hide he beat a yelping retreat, the old coon riding his shoulders for a hundred feet like a fiery leech.

Later in the swart shadows of the tamaracks, Young Specs sat within three feet of the old one as he ate. He was even allowed to mumble over a discarded wing of the hen and cloy his mouth with feathers. Apparently he had not been found wholly wanting and the full mystery of life, or so he then thought, seemed opened to him.

Warm weather came, almost overnight. The hillsides wept freshets, big paint-green frogs held choir practice in a thousand pools, and the greening swamp woods were populous with all manner of coons. And all manner of other creatures, too, all intent on the sweet and secret errands of spring.

The oversized moon they kept in those parts to light love on its way, was a spellbinder, and Young Specs recalled what had gotten him out of bed at least three weeks too soon. He prowled and prowled, by night and by day, knowing only that he must see behind the ranges—must! What he looked for was not clear, but it no longer concerned even the splendid old freebooter by whose side he had fought. Everyone else seemed to know, however; the woods and the very air was prescient with it. The polygamous rabbits knew. Rufa, the dog fox, smiled it at him as he slipped swiftly after his coy red vixen, and the squirrels sitting in their knothole doorways, barked to the world at large that Young Specs, a very great fool who didn't even know what it was all about, was passing on his silly lonely way.

Still, it was three whole weeks before Specs found an answer to it all. She was a small captious creature with a cunning pointed mask and bright canny eyes. She had ideas that leaned toward feminism and there was disdain in her dainty, picking gait. Older than Specs, she led him a chase that was not at all merry before condescending to set up denkeeping. But like all her kind she made life spicy. There was no peace around her, but there were short blissful periods of delight that more than made up for dire discord.

With the coming of late summer all the raccoons in the region began banding together by common accord, for fall is the high time for coons. The frogs and young birds were going now, but there was rich milky corn in the fields of the farmers, to say nothing of chickens. Young Specs' experience had deepened and now he took his place as a proper coon among the big coons of the swamp.

Followed two parlous months of pillage and depredation in which the coon gang of nearly a dozen deviled the dogs of the district and racked their wily brains for new ways of scotching the farmers. Those were the nights! Most of the coons were shrewd, battle-scarred veterans; all of them were born with a hatred of dogs in their blood.

Nightly they raided farmyards and hen roosts; tore down standing corn and climbed orchard trees to fling down apples that they never ate. As the Hunter's Moon began to ride high in the sky a peculiar madness possessed the coon gang, and the more danger attached to their raids the more they loved it.

One frosty night they engineered a nine-foot tunnel and got into the well-stocked cellar of old Deacon Soames, a rich farmer, while the Deacon's chained dog yapped and raved but fifty feet away. He was too used to yapping at the moon, that dog, so nobody paid any attention to him for some time. In the first gray of dawn the Deacon himself looked out of an upstairs window and saw a whole line of coons emerging from the tunnel, loaded down with salt pork, bacon and barreled eels.

Stanch church member that he was, the Deacon's language as he rushed downstairs in his nightshirt almost brought on another hot spell. In the dark he could not locate a gun. Rushing out weaponless he saw the last coon just emerging from the tunnel with half a side of bacon in his jaws. That coon happened to be Specs himself. The Deacon flung himself bodily at him, gripping both hands round the thief's body to hold him down. As long as Specs could get traction he was able to drag the old man along. Notably tightfisted and not overly large, the Deacon hung on and was dragged, nightshirt and all, for forty-five feet by actual count, into the frost-rimed, treble-welted blackness of the hardwoods before he let go.

The incident when related next morning at Hod Archer's store was the cause of the biggest coon hunt of the entire season which took place that night. The Deacon was there with his hound dog, and Sam Wetherwax and old Sol Wire, Al Sloane and the Ballard boys with their two famous coon dogs, faultless trackers. That hunt lasted until dawn. Two coons were treed and done to death and one of them was the grand old boar who had been Specs' initiator. Special luck attended Specs himself. He sought a hollow tree at the first far sound of the dogs and lay quivering while the world howled outside his walls.

Not long after this, fall passed on overnight; a north wind arose at dusk and before morning the forest was white with snow. Specs sought his old den in the ancient oak. His mate had disappeared two days before, and so had most of the other coons of the swamp. The torpor of approaching hibernation was heavy upon him and he would not have pulled the head of the choicest young pullet had it run straight into his paws.

That spring he overslept; in fact, it was an urgent bite from his mate that finally roused him. She had come in search of him, bringing her sheaves with her—four tiny coons, each with a Foxy Grandpa pair of spectacles on his nose, diminutive replicas of Specs himself. Specs wasn't particularly impressed, but as time went on it became evident that they were inexorably attached to his ways and days, the foibles of fatherhood had their way with him.

In the summer following Specs fought his fights with relish and dispatch. No flies settled on him now, nor did anyone knock any chips off his shoulder and get away with it. He was a mature coon now of really remarkable size: twenty-five pounds in weight and nearly three feet long. Few boars could stand up to him. Parenthood wrought in him an inner maturity to match the outer. Most of Specs' strategy came to him instinctively out of the massed wisdom of his kind, who had established the original coon stations in these woods, practiced their banditry, and died before rifles or under the fangs of dogs for centuries. But there were other things he learned through his own boldness and his deathless curiosity.

One late afternoon Specs was cornered in Sam Wetherwax's barn, a big hogshead was thrown over him and a stout timber braced between it and the barn roof to hold him till Sam went to fetch some friends and their dogs. There is a set etiquette to coon hunting, and the law is that only the dogs may do the killing. Even among the pineys and poor whites the rule is rarely broken. Guns are used only to force a treed coon to come down and meet the dogs. Sam wanted more dogs and a friend or two more to share the fun.

When the men returned an hour later, the timber had

fallen and Specs had tunneled to freedom. This Houdini-like performance made the big coon famous throughout the district, for Sam stressed the matter of the dark-ringed spectacles. Old Specs, he was called from then on, hunters taking it for granted he was an old coon because of his craft and size.

By the time fall came again Specs had been seen by at least half a dozen hunters, usually under the most incriminating circumstances—laying waste to some orchard, or just emerging red-handed from a chicken run. He had become a character, and each time a hunter took his dogs out for a night's "shining" he hoped to be the one to hang up Old Specs' hide. But men and dogs continued to match their wits against him in vain, for Specs had become a very Talleyrand of the woods.

One reason for this was that no one had ever discovered Specs' home tree. It was in a hollow high up in an aged oak. The opening was not visible from the ground and from the day his young'uns were able to climb, Specs never allowed any of the family to enter by the front door direct. On going forth or returning he would lead his little following along an arboreal route, from bough to overlapping bough and tree to tree, which no man could find or dog smell out.

As fall drew on again he initiated the family into the dangers of farmyard raids. It was when returning from one of these that they heard the deep-toned yelping bellows of the coon pack coming through the woods, broken through by the shrill whistles of hunters. This hunt was between them and home and was, moreover, one of the big coon hunts of the season. Specs circled, trying to lose the family's trail in a creek, but presently short frenzied yips signaled that the dogs had come upon their fresh trail. And they were coming fast. If the family separated and ran for it, one or two of the youngsters would inevitably be overtaken and killed. If they kept together they would be treed and most of them would surely die. Specs waited till the last minute, then turned back to carry out the immemorial code that male coons have kept for centuries. He would face the pack alone, draw them off and hold them till the family could lose their trails in the river.

So it was that as the first of the dogs, a big liver-and-black hound, came rushing up, a black-masked form hurled itself out of the thickets and wrapped itself about his neck and shoulders like a deadly hood. Specs had learned well the lesson of swift offensive. The surprise of the thing turned the hound's bluster into yelps of dismay. Dirklike teeth met in the nape of his neck and one of his silky ears was torn to ribbons before he broke away. Then the entire pack of six swept up, voicing the short frenzied yaps that meant quarry sighted.

The odds against Specs were overwhelming and no slightest quarter could be expected, yet he did not hesitate. The hard, dilated pupils of his eyes shone like phosphor as he flung himself into their midst, sounding the harsh churring battle cry of his kind. For a time nothing was visible but a whirling, heaving wave of dogs, nose-hubbed. Then the wave broke and the raccoon, still unimpaired, upreared like a young bear just as four hunters came up: Deacon Soames, Doc Eastman and the two Ballard boys, carrying a lantern.

The Deacon had never outlived his belittlement of a year before. As the light showed up the coon's spectacled face he raised his rifle, his white beard jerking furiously. The law of the coon hunt might have been broken then and there had not Doc Eastman jerked the Deacon's gun aside. Then all four men stared dumbly, gripped by the biggest thing in fights they had seen in years.

Specs' tactics were like those of a skilled boxer in a street fracas. He was as hard to hold as quicksilver and again and again he broke seemingly fatal holds by slipping imperceptibly within his loose hide. Making swift dashes to avoid being surrounded, he finally got his back up against a thorny greenbrier where the dogs had to come at him one or two at a time. Within seconds thereafter two of the pack backed away howling, with necks gashed by the coon's razor-edged claws, and paws bitten clean through.

Before the dogs rallied to another attack, Specs in a series of rushes, gained another hundred feet in the direction of the river, with dogs snapping all around him. Low to the ground and perfectly balanced, he ducked, backed and sidestepped with a speed no dog could equal. The blackness of the thickets was all in his favor and dog bit dog without knowing it in the mad melee. When the men with their lanterns caught up they found the coon locked jowl to throat with Baldy, the Ballards' hound and the moving spirit of the pack. As the two threshed about in the thickets, Specs wrapped himself about the dog's neck and head, working dark diableries on windpipe and jugular with his black prying fingers, and when Baldy dragged himself into the bushes, it was to stay.

Still silent and terribly efficient, Specs closed with yet another dog, taking bite after bite from the pack in order to gain the hold he wanted with his forty fighting teeth. The lantern was upset in the flurry and when it was lit again that dog limped to his master with his throat deeply slashed.

Specs was bleeding from a dozen wounds when he made a final stand with his back to a tree. Less than a hundred feet now to the water. The men came running and shouting, trying to head him back. But Specs pulled a surprise charge instead of a retreat. His thick coat bristling until he seemed twice his size and with a dog hanging to his scut of a tail, he dashed between the long legs of Stan Ballard and down to the water.

All the dogs except the Ballard coon hound, Lucy, had had enough by now. When Specs dove into the stream, Lucy sprang in after, wild with killing fury. Instinct told Specs just what to do. As Lucy swam up he whirled and closed with her, climbed upon her head and rode her down. She struggled valiantly, but only succeeded in driving herself deeper.

Specs sank with her, black fingers on her windpipe. When he came to the surface he was alone and the men on the opposite bank heard him bark triumphantly.

"That's him," Stan Ballard said. "Reckon we'll find what's left of Lucy floatin' in the lower crick tomorrow. Next time I let a dog of mine in the water with a coon—I don't!"

Doc Eastman produced a consoling flask. "Two dogs out of business and two dogs killed, out of six—and only one coon," he said. "Boys, I reckon none of us'll live to see a fight like that again. Why, I don't know as we ought to even tell about it! They'll just think we're bigger liars than we are."

As they turned home Steve Ballard spoke: "I don't know but mebbe I wish nobody ever does hang up Old Specs' hide. Sort of a credit to these old woods, he is."

As for Specs, that battle marked the end of current family duties. Two nights later as the full moon rose, he attended the big fall stag party of male coons in the swamp, and took his rightful place as the moving spirit of the gang.

▪ The Keepers of the River Dam

SUMMER HAD GONE, ALMOST OVERNIGHT, AND AUTUMN was on, that rich, golden, and wonderfully silent autumn of the Brunswick forests. Along the Coldwater, the nights were still with knife-edged frosts, and the short days grown mellow as ripened fruit. The little stream, which ran boisterous and gushing in early summer, slipped shrunken and silent now between its banks, under the imminent feel of winter.

Below the hardwood knoll where second-growth birch, poplar, and willow dropped yellowed leaves in the water, the stream ran smooth and clear amber—two rods wide. It was this stretch of still water that a family of beavers had chosen for the site of their winter lodge and storage pool.

In early October, after two years of living in a big hole in the bank under the knoll, the beavers had decided that this was a perfect building spot, and now all night and part of the day their ceaseless labor was in evidence. A dam was in process of building across the river, and the excruciating labor and nicety of judgment involved in anchoring the mud and brushwood barrier against the current would have called forth praise from the most expert engineers. These huge water rats were the most industrious and finished artisans of all the animal world.

There were eight members of the family, the old leader and his mate, four "kits" ranging from one to two years, and an older son and his new-found mate who had not yet broken away from the protection of the family lodge.

Old Keeonek, head of the household, was a patriarch of many summers, wise in craft, extraordinary in size. His flat, whiskered mask was beginning to gray. His cunning and caution were as remarkable as his physique, for in the wilderness no individual reaches great size or age without good cause. He weighed all of fifty pounds and measured three and a half feet, inclusive of his powerful tail, a unique flattened appendage that was put to many remarkable uses: it was a rudder in swimming, a water hammer in the giving of alarms, and in certain instances a weapon and a trowel for his clay masonry.

While the dam was in the making the family lived in the big burrow in the riverbank, entered by secret tunnels under water. Each day two of the family were dispatched into the woods to cut down young trees for the storage pool. It was an eerie sight to see a green tree, after an hour of unseen, unheard labor on the part of the little woodcutters, tremble and sway and come careening down, through no obvious cause, in the midst of the silent wood. Shortly after, it would be trimmed and cut into proper lengths and dragged down cleared pathways to the water's edge, then cleverly anchored butt down in the mud of the pool bottom.

Most remarkable about all the activity of the colony was the uncanny silence with which it was all conducted. The only sounds that would have attracted alien ears were the faint crackle of the young trees as they suddenly leaned and slithered downward. In entering or emerging from the watery element in which they lived, the beavers made no more sound than as if they swam in oil. Their short-napped coats, soft as eider down, well protected by the outer coat of long guard hair, were moisture proof and never soaked through to the skin.

When the dam was finally completed, the water of the stream rose and spread into a spacious pool eight to ten feet deep, and sixty feet wide. Old Keeonek then dove and traversed its length and breadth for final inspection and approval. Allowing for a still greater fall in the water and the sagging of the ice in midwinter, there was yet ample storage room and air space in the pool for the eight keepers of the dam.

Immediately now, at a signal from the patriarch, the eight craftsmen began another stupendous task, the building of a winter lodge at the edge of the pool where the water was shallow. Work in a beaver colony never ceases. No bit of construction is ever quite perfect enough; no dam is ever wholly beyond need of repair; and in between times endless quantities of food-wood must be collected, and a constant watch kept against enemies and against possible threat to the dam, such as drifting logs, the sinister inroads of the water, and the grounding of dead fish, which the beaver loathes.

The base for the huge permanent lodge of the family was laid in the next twelve hours, full twenty feet across. Balls of matted leaves, mud, and sticks were carried throughout the night, seven workers swimming with the endless succession of loads held in their short thick arms and clutched against their breasts, while one of their number was ever on the lookout—a gnomish, whiskered figure sitting upright on the top of the dam with beady eyes that took note of every stirring of leaf or ripple.

With the coming of morning light the work did not stop, for Keeonek had decreed that there be no sleep for the family for a time. There would be time and plenty for rest when the ice spread over the river, but now, by certain signs he recognized, bad weather was imminent.

He was right. Before the work was half completed there came a series of heavy frosts and a light fall of snow. But construction was not held up, for most of the building material, coming from the bottom of the pond, was available in spite of freezing weather.

The first real snow saw the imposing family lodge completed, a circular domelike dwelling five feet in height above the water, having two underwater entrances, one a winding passage that led to the sleeping quarters in the dry upper chamber, the other straight, for the purpose of bringing in food-wood to the lower room. The frost had by now hardened the thick mud and stick walls of the house to iron, so that no enemy could possibly break through. The snow, covering the rough pile, made it look to the unobservant eye like a careless mass of driftwood and brush grounded by the bank.

The big burrow in the riverbank was now deserted, and each of the eight beavers slept in his separately appointed nest in the large upper room of the lodge. These nests were arranged around the opening in the floor to the exit passage, so that any beaver might slip down the passage to the pond below without disturbing the other inmates.

So splendid was the sense of order in the family and so instinctively clean is the beaver clan that there was never any litter or crowding or dispute in the domicile. The aroma of musk and castor, which every beaver carries about him, filled the dwelling at all times with penetrating, antiseptic odors, and a separate chamber had been dug to contain excreta.

It was about this time that the beavers first became aware of the existence of enemies in the vicinity of their new home. The abrupt and unwarned damming up of a forest stream is on a par with setting oneself up as the proprietor of a water hole in a desert land, or the keeper of a tollgate on a highway; it is bound to be hotly contested. In the first place it temporarily diminishes the stream level on the reaches below the dam; then, too, the passage of fish is stopped. But these things the beavers never consider.

A family of otters a mile downstream, finding that the run of fish downriver had suddenly come to a complete stop, set off upstream to investigate the matter. They had a fair idea of what they would find, knowing the ways of the beavers, but being six in number, were not prepared to face the formidable fighting array of old Keeonek's household. They appeared in the beaver pool one afternoon quite suddenly, and with a great turmoil of splashing water and whistled challenges, they mounted the dam. The beavers, resting in their lodge at the time, were awakened by the racket, decided that somebody was put out about something, and rushed to investigate. At sight of their hereditary enemies, the otters, their small eyes glowed red from their blunt, furry faces, and they hurled themselves in a body to the attack.

So fierce was the battle they put up that within five minutes the pool was cleared of the enemy with no particular damage having been wrought. The otters, knowing they were outnumbered, went on their way upstream, mewing over their wounds, leaving the victors scolding excitedly about the dam, examining and re-examining the barricade and spillway for some injury that might have occurred.

This skirmish was but the beginning of a prolonged period of watchfulness and warfare, as the beavers well knew. The feud between the otter and beaver clans is age-old, and as natural and instinctive as that between dog and cat. In the first place, the beaver works all the time and the otter does little but play; the otter is a natural flesh eater, while the beaver is strictly a browser. Moreover, the otter is an incurable vagabond, constantly roaming, while the beaver is fanatical about his home. It is the grasshopper and the ant all over again, only worse, for both these parties must live in the same watery element, and the beaver cannot set up his dam and domicile without cutting off the run of fish and hence the otter's sustenance.

The otters, driven from their favorite haunts downstream, were now forced to resort to a much less favorable habitat upriver, and their rancor grew by slow degrees. For a time the situation had its return for the otters, for the fish, journeying downstream, would come to the barrier of the beaver dam, and except for a few which would slither over the spillway, they would turn about and plunge bewilderedly upstream again. In this condition, even the lightning-swift trout fell easy frey to the otters, and for a few weeks the black fishermen fared very well.

Then came the first bloodshed between the clans. One of Keeonek's young sons met a young otter on the bank below the dam one night and promptly fell upon him. Locked jowl to throat, each with a fatal hold, they threshed and rolled to the water's edge and sank beneath the surface. Their cutting teeth bit momentarily deeper and deeper, for neither would relinquish his hold. In that grim grip they sank for a final time to the bottom and died still locked.

There they rested till the next day, when the lightened bodies rose and floated aimlessly with the current, bumping each other along the swirling eddies as if their war was still on.

It was thus that they were found by Long Tom Handy, the white-haired trapper who lived on the lower branch of the river. Handy read the full story of the quarrel in the torn throats and lacerated pelts, and guessed that this had been only one battle in a bitter war. Handy had always known of the bad blood that existed between beaver and otter, but had never had opportunity to observe the working out of such a feud. Filled with a curiosity of all such secrets of the forest, he set off upstream to locate the beaver colony and find, if possible, the runways of the otters. During the months that followed he became a spectator to many an interesting turn in the prolonged beaver-otter war.

With the last of November, winter, setting in suddenly with fierce frosts, clamped down on the river overnight, binding it with a sheet of ice, transparent and over an inch thick. From now on, the family of beavers would be held virtually prisoners in their winter lodge and pool, dependent wholly on the supply of storage wood they had collected that fall, together with such roots and bulbs as grew in their pool, to tide them through till spring.

Under the biting gales that now blew daily, the forest world surrounding the river grew bleak and frozen hard as iron. Snow swept across the surface of the ice, and up above, the beavers could hear faintly the creaking complaint of swaying trees and wind-tossed branches. But down beneath the protecting ice life moved on as tranquil and ordered as on a spring morning. The weeds swayed softly in the gentle current just as they had in summer, and the beavers swam to and fro in water that was no colder than it had been in autumn. As they moved about at their work, warm and secure, listening to the hard snow slithering across the ice roof of their refuge, the little bead-bright eyes of Keeonek's household seemed to glow with satisfaction over their conscious well-being.

The beaver family now had but one worry, and that had nothing to do with enemies, but with the safety of their dam. Everything depended on that. A break in the dam, even a small leak, in midwinter might prove fatal, for with the ice solid over the river they would be unable to get out and repair the damage. Once the water of their pool went down their precious supply of food-wood would be frozen into an iron mass at the bottom, and even their exit tunnels blocked with ice.

And so, day and night, the beavers listened for any change in the restful tune of the water sliding over their spillway. Week in and week out they were lulled to sleep by its quiet rhythm, for it told them at any and all hours that all was well.

But there came a day when there was a break in the tune. A violent splashing was heard by one of the beavers who happened to be outside the dam. It brought the other beavers swiftly from the mouth of the lodge, to go rushing up and down the length of the dam in the underwater gloom to locate the possible danger. It happened that the otters, who roam the upper ice and snow in winter as freely as the waterways beneath, had journeyed downstream, and coming upon the open water below the dam, stopped to play. Of course they knew they could do no damage to the huge frozen mass, but they clambered up and down over the face of the barrier, peering in every cranny and sniffing at every branch and twig. The beavers, not knowing what might be threatening the dam, put in a terrible hour before they realized the cause of the splashing.

Thereafter, almost daily, the otters would come down

to the open water to play. They made an icy slide down the steep bank into the water, and down this they would slither, legs doubled under them, ending in a thrilling plunge to the bottom of the pool. They pursued this game with the glee of small boys sliding downhill. On each occasion the beavers heard them without, and their initial terror was renewed, while their hatred for the otters grew. By mid-January the river had sunk to its lowest level and the ice sagged in midstream. The fish now, thanks to the otters' deadly skill, were scarcer and scarcer, and the time came, through famine and necessity, when the feud of the two clans was brought to a queer issue. By February the otters, who had been ranging far up and down the river, were forced to seek fish in the beavers' deep pool, where many wary fish had gone for safety. Swifter and more agile in the water than the beavers, the otters would watch their chance and dart in and out for fish. Thus the skirmishing became almost incessant, for the beavers always gave chase.

The climax to the feud came about quite naturally and inevitably; what was done was unpremeditated on the part of the otters, but to the beavers it was the one heinous and unforgivable offense. The littering of their pool about its edges with fish scales and fins that had floated downstream, the beavers had endured for weeks, much as they detested the smell of fish, but when it came to defiling the interior of their dwelling with such refuse their rage knew no bounds.

It happened in this way. A particularly agile trout had craftily taken refuge in the deep water surrounding the beaver lodge, and had long eluded all attempts of the otters to catch him. But Tunawa, the big leader of the otter family, slipping into the pool one day at a time when the beavers were all at rest in their lodge, captured this shiny fellow after a breath-taking chase. Almost at the limit of his wind by the time he made the capture, Tunawa, instead of swimming back upstream to the nearest breathing place, dove with a rush straight into the entrance of the beaver lodge with his prize. He emerged in the vacant lower chamber and, halting to regain his breath, fell to eating on the spot.

The beavers, roused by the commotion, started cautiously down the narrow passage from the upper room, but before a single animal could emerge, Tunawa had blocked the way. Extraordinarily large for one of his clan, he was more than a match for any member of the household save Keeonek himself. Fiercely hungry, unmindful of the wrathful mutterings from the passage ahead, he humped his back and bolted fish, hissing and snarling warnings between mouthfuls. There was room in the upper passage for only one animal at a time and the lower end of it was blocked by Tunawa with the four-pound bulk of the trout.

Before old Keeonek had generated the wrath to hurl himself to a precarious attack, Tunawa had bolted his fill, and turning, dove like a plummet to the safety of the stream, leaving behind him the stenchful mess of scales, slime and fins, to litter the beaver's scrupulously clean dwelling. That litter, furthermore, abomination that it was, could not be dumped from the lodge, which had but an underwater entrance, but must be taken up in the teeth of the enraged householders and carried out to be buried in mud or set afloat in the stream.

Five lengths behind the disappearing otter, Keeonek's bulk plopped into the water of the lower exit. His six followers came close behind him and the whole seven, shooting like projectiles from the lodge entrance, took up the chase of the fleeing despoiler. Nor did the chase end at the pool limit. The last notch had been reached, the crowning insult suffered, and only the annihilation of the otter clan could pay for it.

Long Tom Handy, happening to pass by the dam some ten minutes previous, had seen the faint commotion beneath the ice of the pool, caused by Tunawa's capture of the silver trout. A month before he had cut a square hole in the pond ice, into which he had lowered a covered box with a glass bottom. Creeping silently up to this spy hole, he had often watched the activities of the beaver colony. Pausing on this day, he knelt to catch a glimpse of what might be taking place below.

He had waited but a minute or two when he saw the dark, sinuous form of Tunawa, the otter, shoot across his range of vision, followed quickly by all seven of the keepers of the river dam. Fugitive and pursuers disappeared upstream in a swirl of foam and bubbles. Handy foresaw that this chase would end in drama. When, after he had waited five or ten minutes, the beavers did not return, his guess seemed more than ever likely. Rising, the old woodsman made his way upstream toward the otter's stronghold, keen for some idea of the outcome of the affair.

Tunawa, with his flying start, had outdistanced his pursuers. Two hundred yards upstream he came to rest in a dome-shaped ice cave under a hummock where the expanding ice crowded upward over a half-submerged rock, making a roomy chamber. But less than a minute had passed when around the bend in the stream came Keeonek and his family, swimming four abreast and churning the water fiercely. Tunawa took one look at their ferocious masks and read there the denouement of his day's hunt. There was the flash of white fangs beneath his catlike drooping whiskers and a low churring growl like the ominous note of a saw biting through timber—that was his acceptance of the showdown. Neither panicky nor perturbed, he glared back a challenge, then sped upstream to warn his household.

The coming clash would be a grim battle in which the otters would be outnumbered, but it found no craven strain in their courage. There was never a thought of flight; for in spite of their many crimes, no member of the weasel tribe was ever known to lack craft or fierceness in battle. Savage hate but no fear showed in the usually bright inquisitive eyes of the five big otters as they made their final stand about the open water of a spring hole, where a tiny creek flowed into the main stream.

The seven besiegers arrived on the scene with a rush that sent the water washing up the bank, breathless from their long chase. For a moment or two they stopped, eying the other clan from a distance of four or five feet, eyes glowing like coals with a contained rage and enmity. Each clan saw a deadly foe in every member of the other.

It was the big leading otter that gave some signal for attack, perhaps with an idea of forcing the issue while the beavers were still winded. The five closed with the seven in darting snakelike rushes at the water's edge, and the surface of the pool was lashed to frenzy as five pairs of fighters locked together. The two young beavers thus left out, rushed here and there through the water, seeking a telling grip on one or other of the assailants.

Out on the snowy bank and then down into the icy depths of the pool the struggle waged, stark murder in the heart of every fighter. Snow-white fangs snicked and the hue of the swirling water here and there deepened to a brickish stain in the open pool.

Old Keeonek's initial attempt to close with the leader of the otters had failed. With a troutlike flick, the weasel chief had eluded him to close with the beaver's eldest son, not through any faintheartedness, but with crafty intent to make one or two swift kills and lessen the odds against his household. Keeonek, seeing this pair sink beneath the surface, closed with a young female otter. The kills of the two clan leaders were timed the same, almost to the second, and as each rose, panting and victorious, another pair of young fighters, locked in a fatal throathold that would never be broken, were sucked under the downstream ice, thus adding the number of slain to four, within the space of five minutes.

At this moment the mates of the two leaders, locked in furious combat, sank in the middle of the pool, and each of the big males rushed toward the spot in a surge of rage, met each other midway, and the battle royal was on. They came together with the speed of sharks, with ripping throat slashes; twisted aside, and turned again, feinting like skilled duelists. Each was keen for the final killing grip.

Though Keeonek possessed the greater bulk, and the greater crushing power of jaw, Tunawa was his master in swiftness, and his the longer and sharper teeth. Again and again the otter struck with lancelike swiftness, while Keeonek, still the more contained, bided his time. Then Tunawa, overhasty and desperate in the knowledge that his family was outnumbered, made the mistake that could not be undone. His jaws closed on Keeonek's shoulder and instead of releasing again, clamped spasmodically.

Keeonek spun round, stiffening his powerful spine to an arch of whalebone. Tunawa's fangs tore loose and for a moment gripped only a mouthful of loose hide. In that moment Keeonek achieved a neckhold at the base of the other's jaw, and his powerful teeth worked inexorably in and in toward the jugular.

Tunawa's grip released; his keen, vindictive fangs struck

in one last attempt. His long neck arched outward and his jaws closed in as near a vital grip as he could gain—the pouchlike bulge at the side of Keeonek's fat chops. They closed and set fast in a grip that not even death could loosen, for already death was near. In utter silence, down in the choking depths, the pair writhed and whirled about, eyes closed now, the one in his final throes, the other blinded by the roiled and bloody water. In his last spasms the otter's lithe body twisted about his assailant like a snake, claws ripping, but his steel-like jaws remained locked, even after death had touched him.

With lungs and eyeballs close to bursting from the prolonged strain, Keeonek loosed his jaws and put forth the last of his reserve to gain the life-giving air once more. But the heavy body of Tunawa now hung like a millstone from his neck, weighting him down. Before he could labor to the surface the current had caught them both in its swing and carried them under the ice.

Desperately the big beaver breasted the current, alternately stopping to tear at his enemy's weight. He had paid off his score with the otter, and the dam was now safe, though his own life seemed the forfeit. Now the unexpected happened. The swirling bodies bumped against something in midcurrent—the rock on which Tunawa had paused in his flight upstream. Keeonek half grounded against it, and paused, his claws rasping vainly for a hold on the icy surface. Then a movement from above.

Keeonek's mate, after worsting the she-otter, had landed there gasping, to regain her strength, only seconds before. Now as her reeling senses took in the situation she rallied and went plunging bravely to the rescue. Like a young alligator at a carcass, she fastened upon Tunawa's jaws and tugged and jerked till teeth and hide gave way, and old Keeonek, patriarch of the river, was freed.

Together the keepers of the river dam crawled out on the flat-topped rock, where long and long they rested in the blessed air, doctoring their own and each other's wounds.

Tom Handy had arrived at the open spring hole that had been the scene of the battle just in time to see the final skirmish between the younger members of the two clans. The remaining beavers had driven the two surviving otters out of the water and up the snowy bank as Handy came silently up. The otters were slowly retreating into the woods where the beavers dared not follow. On the bank of the pool lay the dead female otter and it was plain to the old woodsman what trend the battle royal must have taken. As he came up the three young beavers suddenly whirled and plunged from sight in the pool, while the two otters melted away in the darkening woods.

"Well, Keeonek and his family have won the feud," Handy told himself as he knelt to remove the pelt of the dead she-otter. "And a good thing all round," he added, "for there's no thriftier tribe in the woods."

In his admiration Handy elected then and there that Keeonek and his colony should go free of any traps of his from this time on.

▪ Injun Devil

A DIM GHOSTLAND OF ONE ENDLESS HORIZON—AS FAR AS THE eye could sweep, on every side stretched a limitless snow expanse, and there was only a slight added levelness to show where the tundra merged into the ice fields of the unnamed Arctic bay. Far out, where the restless floes heaved and split against the fixed ice of the shore line, crouched the spirit of the region. Splatted shapeless against the ice at the edge of the open water, the huge polar bear might have been taken for one of the tossed-up ice hummocks that rose about her.

Motionless she waited, her narrow, black-tipped muzzle pointed out across the swirling waters. On the edge of a great floe the dark figure of a bearded seal stood out. It was less than a hundred yards distant, but the little reddish eyes of the polar could hardly make it out. As usual, her keen, wet nose told the story.

But even more nearsighted than the polar was the old seal. He trusted to his ear and to submarine vibrations for safety and prey. Out in the open water to the leeward of the seal's floe, a small ice cake was floating among the many big "pans." This particular ice cake kept to the line of white-caps breaking against the far side of the floe. Strangely it was not tossed by the waves, but seemed to have a will of its own. When it was just abreast of the seal's floe, it suddenly sank. A minute later from out the white smother of spray almost beneath the bull seal's nose, there arose the startling head and shoulders of a second polar bear.

The great floe rocked as the bear kicked his nine-foot mass up on the ice. Cut off from the water, the bull seal wheeled and scuttled across the ice on spasmodic flippers. Doubling himself in two incredible lunges the bear was upon the seal before he gained the water. A darting paw scooped the wriggling prize upon its its back. Then resting his forefeet upon the kill, the male bear sent a hoarse grunting cough across the ice pans to his mate.

Already she had slid forward and was swimming toward him through the black swirling water. Together on the rocking floe they feasted off the catch. There was hardly a perceptible difference between the two, except that the coat of the male was a trifle shaggier and his was the greater length of head and jaw.

It was the she-bear that first withdrew from the feast. The wind was rapidly increasing to a gale from the northwest. Daily the stretch of open water had been narrowing. Far out, the driving scud on the bay veiled the yellowish light in the south, so that strange shadows lay crimson across the snow. From underneath the ice fields came a dull booming and the whole expanse of ice heaved and quivered restlessly, expectantly. It was the first of the October gales from the Arctic. Already sleet was in the air.

Something of the heaving uneasiness of the ice fields was tossing within the old she-bear. To the edge of the floe she shambled and stood looking off across the angry waters, her narrow black-muzzled head rocking up and down and swinging slightly at each descent, describing a U in the air.

It all came to her down the wind; the great snows were at hand. The high wild screaming of Arctic gulls and willicks told of the massing and drilling for the Labrador flight.

Pivoting on her ungainly hind legs she moved back to her mate who was coughing over the dry whiskers of the bearded seal. She laid her muzzle on his shoulder and low talk passed between them, almost inaudible, like the sounds which escape a dog's mouth when he yawns. Turning with one accord, they swam back to the stationary ice of the shore line, where the Madame again tested the wind, while the old male sat on his haunches and approved.

It was settled in a few minutes. The female was heavy with young this fall, and now of all times must she and her whims dictate. Loath to leave the seal grounds, she had stayed on week after week. The cutting wind now admonished her to move south for the good of the cubs yet unborn. Shoulder to shoulder the two stood for another short interval on the edge of the ice, ruffing each other's necks and shoulders. Gently the old male bunted her fat side; then as with one thought, they wheeled about on their hindquarters and shambled off, the female taking the south bend of the bay, the male northward, where he would spend a more or less sleepless winter stalking seal among the bergs and ice fields at the top of the world.

Southward along the east shore of Hudson's Bay Madame held her course, traveling at a loose, shambling gait which knew no fatigue. The water on her shaggy coat had mixed with the driving snow and frozen, forming an armor of ice-crust about her body. Besides being a protection, she utilized this as a means of locomotion, sliding down ice hummocks on her haunches and the under part of her forelegs with a comical ungainly joy. There was speed to that lumbering pace in spite of the loafing ease of the movements.

For two days she stopped neither for food nor sleep. This great padded creature had been whelped upon fresh blood and seal meat; all her life she had eaten meat that still quivered with life. Incredible stores of vitality were acrawl in her sliding muscles.

The third day found her beyond the Height-Of-Land, almost to the tree line. By now the permanent slate-black clouds of winter darkened the sky to the north and west. They were far and mackereled, like banks of corrugated metal, and told of a winter of more than ordinary severity. In the low-lying valley of the Anninuik her march ended, where a line of dunes and ledges of curious painted rock marked the shoreline of an ancient sea.

Here in a snowdrift among the rugged rocks she curled up for the long winter sleep, letting the snow cover her as it would. Three days later the ceaseless Arctic storms were raging over the Barren Grounds and Madame was sleeping in a cave under three feet of snow. Once only her rest was broken within the next month, and then it was to give birth to two whimpering cubs. Four hours in all she was awake, coaching her little ones in the baffling knack of nursing; then slept again, conserving all her vitality for the young. In usual course, they would sleep and feed the winter months away; grow fat while the mother fell gaunt and lean. Food was all she need supply. The snow, topped with an iron crust, would protect them; and the rising heat from her great body, which had already melted a sizable cave about them, could be trusted to keep an air hole open through the snow, until the warm winds of spring set them free.

Many miles to the south of the Anninuik, in the heart of a tamarack swamp, there had been another parting of mates that fall. A pair of carcajous, the giant wolverines of the north, had gone their divided ways after a pitched battle. Known to trappers as Injun Devil, Glutton, Bad Dog, and North Shore Devil, the carcajou is of all animals the most hated and loathsome. Indians say he is a fiend with a life-long feud against man and all below. Neither man nor beast will eat of his musky meat; when he is killed it merely means a robber of food and trap lines has been done away with, for his coarse ragged hide, which seems ever in a state of molting, is practically worthless.

In reality Injun Devil is a cross, related to many a robber of the weasel persuasion, to all the musk-carrying polecats that ever tainted fresh air—a mongrel that has inherited the evil of all parties and the quality of none—unless one counts his nerve. He certainly had nerve as must all things that live outside the law.

The arrival of a pair of unsavory sons late that summer had likewise to do with the parting of the Injun Devils. Thereafter the she-carcajou, who had long been on mere snapping terms with her mate, refused to allow him within ten rods of the home den. The ultimate pitched battle al-luded to ended in the male taking himself off to the north, leaving his young and herself, with a slashed hide, to roam the tamarack swamp undisturbed.

Northward the old male traveled, following what im-pulse who can tell. Something in his flat head called to winter it up among the stunted trees. Beyond the poplar, beyond the burr oak, beyond the white and the red pine belts, beyond even the willow and the little yellow birches he wandered, to that dim ghostland of half-lights where the creeping juniper and dwarfed spruce cling close to the ground and grow bent and twisted in the ceaseless gales that blow over the Barren Grounds. There, at the edge of the treeless plains, where the coarse northern moss hangs in gnarled beards from the junipers, he made his winter quarters in a rock den.

For a week or two the old carcajou waxed fat. The wanton snowshoe rabbit still thronged the thickets; also there were grouse, northern ptarmigan, and stoats that had never known the devilish cunning of Injun Devil in smelling out forms and burrows. Stalking and surprise were the carcajou's game. He never ran anything down, but lived by thievery. Endowed with a body greater by five times than the largest of his marten ancestors, and possessing all the acuteness of six senses in proportion, his game was cunning and a slow, heavy strength.

Out on the marshy flashlets of the Barrens thousands of wild fowl still moored, staying until the last moment over the strong feeding on the northland bulbs and tubers. In that blackest hour before the dawn, when even the watch of the wild goose grows lax, the carcajou surprised many a meal among the rushes. And the lusciousness of those geese was something he had never dreamed could exist—outside of cat meat, which was his favorite abandonment.

During the third week things changed. The wild birds decamped overnight, and next day began the first of the winter storms. For three days it raged out of the north, scarring the very face of the snows. During that time the carcajou stuck to his den and lived on nothing at all. Venturing forth on the fourth day he found that even the grouse and ptarmigan had disappeared. Although he stalked all that day, nothing went to weight his belly but a stoat and that was but a mouthful or two and had a taste like rawhide gone rancid. Even the mice had burrowed too deep for the grubbing. Arctic hare were plentiful, and the little northern lemming, but living there in the haunts of the quick-pounc-

ing gyrfalcon, these were not to be surprised by the logy
and bear-muscled.

That night came a second storm, and passing, it left behind a cold beyond anything the old carcajou had ever experienced—a still cold. The phlegmatic Injun Devil quickened his patent slow pace to a curious double shuffle and
stopped often to raise his head and work his black cleft in
awe at the unearthly calm that had settled over the land.
The snap of a twig carried a quarter of a mile. That night
the frost probed into the hearts of the juniper and black
spruce until they cracked and groaned aloud.

The uneasiness of the marauder increased. It had not al-
together to do with the cold; he was more immune to that
than even the white wolves of the Barrens. It had to do with
his stomach. His appetite, ever most amazing, had grown
to a monster that let him neither sleep nor rest.

With the coming of the second storm all the snowshoe
rabbits had mysteriously disappeared—as rabbits will. And
they were the main source of food for every meat eater
within the tree limit. Dread clutched at the carcajou's heart.
He must change his hunting grounds at once. But it was
plain that the famine was over all that territory. The hunger
call of the wolves sounded nightly. Twice one afternoon
he ascended a snowy ridge to raise his flat black head and
cast about to the four quarters for the feel of the call.
Strangely enough, it came again from the north.

He started at once. Out across the white expanse of the
tundra he went at his characteristic shuffle; he hurried for
no living thing. His fastest pace was a curious shuffle, not
a trot or a walk, rather a slouch; its one quality, tirelessness.
His shoulders lurched with a ruffianly swagger; he carried
an open insult for all and loafed before the mightiest. Out

in the open his one care was the wolf packs, but he lived by taking chances.

He had traveled steadily, ascending the western rise of the Height-Of-Land, when over a ridge his acute ear caught a curious sound. It was a clicking sound unlike anything he had ever heard, and a smell came with it, a delicate warm scent, like deer. It was faint, a mere taint on the rare air. Only the keenest of the wet-nosed animals could have detected it at all. The carcajou moistened his cleft again and again to get the clearer story, working himself toward the top of the ridge.

Over the ghost-lighted tundra from the north came band after band of caribou, their legions stretching away as far as Injun Devil could see. They were gaunt and aged-looking, almost white, and might have been taken for the spirits of the Barrens, had it not been for the curious travel grunt that came from every animal, seemingly in time to his pace, like the low *whush* from the paunch of a saddle horse going at a trot. It was "la foule" of the Barren Ground caribou, that great yearly migration to the edge of the tree line, mysterious and inevitable as the movement of the planets.

Crouched behind a snow-covered boulder, the carcajou waited, dirty-eyed. Their numbers were incalculable. They came on, twenty or thirty abreast, their long necks pointing straight south. Their faces were white and ancient; long white beards waved under their chins, and their antlers were gnarled like dead tree limbs. The low sounds now became the clacking of hoofs, as if every animal wore shoes with loose, flapping soles.

Many bands had passed before Injun Devil moved from behind his boulder. He was desperate now, maddened by the warm scent of meat. Irresistibly he was drawn nearer and nearer the drifting herds. They showed no alarm and looked neither to the right nor left. The carcajou's teeth bared in a snarl, in defiance of the puniness he felt beside these majestic striding crusaders. But the thicker scent overruled that. He was in the ranks. The slashing hoof of a bull sent him spinning back with a gashed shoulder. No altering of the pace, no deviation of the course, merely a closing up of the ranks. Once more, the blood madness lunged him in. His ribs were all but staved by a descending hoof. There was no breaking that formation to the young that were bunched in the middle.

For nearly twenty-four hours the frozen earth rang like iron under the countless hoofs. All that time the carcajou moved along the fringe of the ranks—unquenchable hatred and lust in the eyes of that black, low-swinging head—a demon ignored by these giants obsessed with the spirit of passage.

"La foule" had drifted into the south and with it had gone the last of the daylight from the Barrens. Thereafter only the pale shimmer of the aurora would be seen, and the weird crimson changing shadows that reflected across the snows from over the rim of the world. . . .

A different warm scent came up to the carcajou's nose. He had been traveling northward but keeping to the trail of the caribou. He had reached the western bend of the An-ninuik, known as the plains of the painted rocks. . . . This scent—it was very curious. It was not caribou—warm and stronger than any trail. He found a hole in the snow. The crust had been broken through by the feet of the herd. Somewhere beneath the snow was fresh meat.

Desperately he clawed at the opening, cutting through snow ice hard as flint. A big slab tore loose. He wrenched it back, slipped and fell headfirst into the dark hole, bringing up with a harsh snarl against the body of the she-polar, who slept with her two cubs cradled between her vast bowed legs.

Madame was deep in the second month of her hibernation. She merely turned a bit in her sleep and moaned. But the cubs were already awake and whimpering. The carcajou fastened himself to their throats, one after the other, until their whimpering ceased. The huge white sleeper stirred uneasily; the preyer crouched, prepared to fight to the death, but she relapsed again. He longed to slash her great throat while she slept, but he knew well the demon that rages in the heart of a she-bear with a dead cub. For the present he was doing well. Hers was a low, deathlike stupor.

He fell to gorging then and there; some fifteen pounds of raw meat he stowed away before he was appeased. Then following the bestial inventiveness of his polecat ancestry, he "musked down" the remainder of the kill. No other living thing would eat of that meat.

Deadened by feeding, it was all the marauder could do to clamber out of the hole. He lurched away among the rocks to rest and doze, drawn by the stupor that follows a gorging.

A half hour after he had disappeared, the cold and the abhorrent stench had done their work. A low sound, between a growl and a moan, issued; then up out of the hole in the snow reared the gaunt white avenger. Her little deep-sunken eyes showed red as she swung her head about into the four quarters, voicing a sort of bleat that held something of elemental agony.

Then she had picked up the scent and was shambling after Injun Devil. The hide hung loose on her gaunt frame for she had not tasted food for two months. Still there were inexhaustible coils of energy stored up in those great gliding muscles. Nothing but death would turn her from that trail.

The carcajou roused from sleep, saw the white shadow of the avenger against the leaden sky. She was moving silently over a ridge he had recently crossed, head swung low, nose to the trail.

Furtively he moved off through the rocks, completing a tangled circle back to the whale-backed ridge she had just quitted. The hide crawled on his back as he came upon her great footprints. He was racking his wily brain for some ingenious trick to escape the mother's wrath. Among the trees he could have eluded her, but here there was nothing for it but to keep moving, and she could tire him out in the end.

Abruptly he flattened himself to the snow. Out on the tundra, coming along the caribou trail was the figure of a big white wolf, and he knew the way of the white wolves of the Barrens. Behind that one was probably a file. He watched intently, his head clearing rather than muddling under the strain.

A turn in the trail showed a pack of seven, trotting in single line. He saw them stop at the polar's den, saw the effect of the musk upon them. Gaunt and hungry as they were, they would not touch the polluted meat in the hole.

The leader yapped a signal and the pack swept forward. The carcajou knew not whether it was his trail or the bear's they followed, but he did know that the hatred of wolves for the carcajous was deep as instinct. If they were after him, it was merely to pay off an old grudge. No wolf would eat of his musky flesh. But the wolves were hungry. And the bear meant meat!

Desperate, the carcajou circled around the ridge, crossed his former trail, then made off at a tangent among the rocks.

This was not the first time he had found himself pitted against great odds. Cold and deadly, his cunning was working. Cornered hate was the outward showing of it, not a sign of a diffusing fear.

A minute later the bear rounded a table of rock, and sensing his fresher trail, lumbered away on it. The carcajou showed himself for a brief instant, then clambered onto a ledge of rock to wait. . . . He had tarried until the last moment. Instinct had told him that. Already the wolves were yapping on the tangled trail. They would arrive but a few moments behind the polar.

Flattened on his ledge, the usually heavy eyes of the carcajou glowed bright. Already Madame was at the base of the ledge, when around the last turn in the trail came the pack. They ran silently now, bunched together as one. The outcome depended upon them. Would the old grudge prove stronger than hunger? Could they pull the white she-monster down if they tried?

Seven silent gray-white devils leaped out of the shadows upon the flanks of the she-bear as she rose on her hind-quarters against the ledge. What followed was a heaving, swaying hell below in the dim shadows, and out of it rose snarls, bellowing, and the horrid click of snapping teeth. The old enemies had been turned into a rescue party. His opponents were at one another's throats.

The polar shook free of the pack again and again, struggling with one-pointed madness to reach the crouching form of the carcajou on top of the ledge. It was booked, however, for Injun Devil to preside over the carnage, the center of which should have been his rent and mangled remains.

The polar's great strength and weight could not avail against that nimble-footed circle. Only when she reared up on her hindquarters did the pack give way. But the moment she dropped to all fours again the tormentors leaped in.

Motionless, pressed against the rock above, the carcajou watched until the great shaggy female was pulled down beside the two still wolves that already lay there. Then the squat form of the robber moved across the ledge and down the opposite side. As the deep, throaty, fighting snarls of the pack subsided to an intermittent snapping and bickering over the kill, Injun Devil skirted off through the rocks toward the den in the snow where the "doctored" bear cubs lay.

▪ Monarch of the Lagoons

ONE SPRING MORNING JUST AFTER A SLUICING FLORIDA downpour, one of the strangest of all wilderness children was born in a cool green nursery among the lily stalks of a wine-brown lagoon. His mother was a cautious old cow of the great interrelated family of manatees who every summer peopled the neighboring ponds and streams, and left mysteriously each fall. She had the graying whiskers and the lined and shriveled countenance that denote age in a manatee as they do in a human.

This new water baby was one of the queerest spectacles in all nature. Seeing him you would never have known what he was, unless you were one of the "fern jumpers" or backwoods crackers who inhabited this amphibious region. He was three feet long and covered all over from his queer round head to his spadelike tail with thick, wrinkly skin resembling elephant hide. He had no teeth yet, but his cleft, purselike upper lip was already beginning to sprout whiskery hairs. With his small eyes closed and his flippers folded together, he looked like a fat fish with a wrinkled dog face. He was in reality as nearly half fish and half mammal as it is possible to become.

Thousands of years ago, before the Second Ice Age, the

dim ancestors of the manatees—strange browsing, land-running animals with four short legs—were driven to take to the water to escape their many carnivorous enemies of the jungles. Throughout the ages nature had indulged the drastic change to the limit of her power. The manatee in time became a water creature, but his lungs are still the lungs of a mammal, and every few minutes he must come up for air. His flat flexible flippers are merely thumbless swimming mittens grown about a pair of short arms.

Born almost in the water, the new fish-mammal infant could swim and float from the moment he came into the world. Within the first twenty-four hours of life his mother took him in her arms and gave him his first trip through the water. He was a solemn, serious little creature and though none of his elders knew it, he was almost a third larger than any day-old manatee had a right to be. Also, instead of being a dull slate-gray color, he was a study in gunmetal and brown, for his father was the big dark-colored bull who had been the acknowledged leader of all the sea cows in the region for as long as any of the backwoodsmen could remember.

It had been a hard year for the sea cows. Death had dogged them every hour of every day. Negro and white hunters had of late been decimating their numbers for their tender veal-like meat, which they salted down like beef for winter use, and for their valuable oil, which all druggists were willing to buy. Crafty river alligators and big garfish of the lagoons had taken to lying in wait for the young ones each spring and, added to this, a sudden cold spell the fall before had killed some of the herd, for all manatees are extremely susceptible to cold.

Unlike their long-tusked cousins, the dugongs of Australia, the manatees were mild and inoffensive by nature, and had no other defense than their size and bulk. In their ever-recurring and age-old battle for existence they faced extinction. Government, awakening tardily to the value of these gentle animals and the interest they lent to the Florida coast, was beginning to take steps for their protection, but it was still a tossup whether this northern species would survive man's avarice and rapacity.

So it was that the newborn manatee in Santee Lagoon was predestined for adventure and vicissitudes. They began on the day of his birth, and continued in swift grim sequence throughout the first year of his life—some of them long, slow, and grilling, others swift and unforeseen as flashes of jagged lightning in a night sky. But the little calf was both luckier and tougher than most of his fellows for he survived all encounters, and in so doing he drew upon the massed wisdom of his race and developed a cunning far beyond his years.

He spent the first few weeks almost constantly with his mother, wrapped in the protecting folds of her flippers, but he could not be there all the time, and those young of the water folk who stray but a few yards from their mothers often never return. It was during the first twenty-four hours of his life as he was floating on his back with his round head just showing above the surface of the water that one of the swiftest deaths that menaced the bayou dwellers struck a blow that almost made the youngster's first day his last. His mother, after scanning the surface of the lagoon for the forty or fifty feet which was the limit of the manatee's vision, and listening intently with a pair of microphone eardrums second to none in the wild, decided there was no danger near. Over the still surface of the lagoon gnats hummed peacefully, gaudy dragonflies glittered and skimmed, and the stillness was intensified by the braying of the big paint-green frogs which inhabited the shallows and whose silence was the chief danger signal for all water dwellers. The mother manatee sank to the bottom where grew the lush reeds and grasses sea cows love to eat.

From mid-sky the telescope eye of a white-headed eagle caught the movement of the little manatee in the shallows. Folding his wings he shot downward, doubtless taking the little swimmer for a big fish basking lazily on the surface. His black-gold eyes were hard and fixed as agates as he hurtled downward without a sound save for the wind whistling through his tail feathers.

Not until the shadow of the bird fell upon him did the nearsighted calf have warning of danger. Immediately he submerged, but slowly like a submarine. In a shower of spray the eagle's talons struck deep into the youngster's sides, locking in the fishhook hold of his kind. Not until then did the sky king realize his mistake; his talons clutched no fish but a mammal, and they had penetrated so deeply that he would be several minutes in extricating them. Young as he was, the calf's weight was too much for the great bird to raise from the water. Though he struggled with wildly flapping pinions he could do no more than raise the youngster to the surface.

The mother manatee came speeding up from the bottom and folded her calf close in her armlike flippers to still his piteous bleating. Minus any means of offensive, the cow simply sank with her little one, dragging the eagle with her. He was a full minute under the water before he extricated his claws and went flapping and splashing shoreward, the most bedraggled and unkingly of birds.

The cow manatee comforted her little one. Balancing on her tail at the bottom of the lagoon, she stood in an upright position, swaying gently to and fro, amazingly like a human mother holding her child, her blunt mask reflecting a look of love and thankfulness. It was thus that the fable of mermaids had its origin, when mariners of ancient times brought home tales of strange sea creatures who nursed their young on the surface of the ocean.

The fierce fright and narrow escape that marked his first day of life were of vital import in developing the early caution which was to be the chief factor in carrying the young manatee through the most dangerous months of calfhood as well as the most perilous year the herd had known. Thereafter he was ever on the alert for danger, especially from above. In the next two weeks the youngster showed an amazing growth, his little eyes became clearer and more distinct, long hairs began sprouting out on his body, and he cut seven blunt pebbly teeth.

Then began a terrible time for the herd. There came a week of torrential rains. Each day the intermittent downpours continued, until all the lagoons were overflowing and the knees of the cypresses and the sprawly spotted sycamores around their margins were submerged in water. Soggy bottoms became pools and ponds, and new waterways reached out like tentacles through the dripping woods. And in the wake of the floods came a new enemy.

The river alligators, who for years had not ventured so far from the larger streams, now came sliding along all the waterways in search of new and unwary hunting. Between darkness and daylight one night a dozen or more of them ensconced themselves in the nearby lagoons and along the reed-grown peninsulas, where they lay camouflaged like dead logs grounded by the floods. Many an incautious one next day went forth and never returned, having come within the eight-foot area of some waiting 'gator's tail stroke.

Twice during the month the saurians remained, death all but had the little manatee. Once, as he lay napping no more than ten feet from his browsing mother, there came a sudden horrid rush from the reeds and a half-grown alligator had the youngster's tail in his jaws. There began then a ghastly tug of war with the 'gator on one side and the mother manatee on the other, the bleating calf the bone of contention between them. The 'gator could have won by simply maintaining a hold with his traplike jaws whose grip the cow manatee had no means of breaking. But when the cow heaved her clumsy body full upon him the saurian made the mistake of losing his temper as well as his hold. For a space his jaws slashed at the she-manatee in punishing rage, but those moments were enough to enable the calf to escape to the bottom. Formidable as the 'gator was, he could not overpower the ten-foot bulk of the big cow; yet with savage tenacity he hung on until he was finally scraped off against the roots of a big sycamore which twined over the opening of one of the refuge dens under the bank which every manatee family maintains.

The second time the calf was caught was as he swam down into the deepest part of the lagoon. Here as he fed in the reflected greenhouse light a grotesque and horrible form emerged from the waving water grass. A pair of slit goatlike eyes gleamed with a gray-green light and a huge dragonlike form came shooting straight at the little manatee.

This time it was no half-grown 'gator, but a wise old mugger with an eleven-foot body like re-enforced armor plate. With all the strength of his tail and flappers the youngster swam shoreward. Twice the jaws of the monster snapped at his tail and twice he flicked instinctively aside as the double rows of interlocking teeth just grazed him.

The third time he was gripped and held as he gained the shallows.

Already the cow manatee had rushed to the scene, and there began one of those pitiful dramas which occur so often in the lives of these mild grass-eating folk. Round and round the mugger swam the frenzied mother, biting ineffectually with her blunt teeth while in her flat mask was mirrored that love and anguish possible only to mammal mothers whose young are born of their bodies, not of egg or spawn.

Foot by foot the scaly monster dragged his prize back toward the deep water, his pale goatish eyes with their vertical pupils seeming to take no note of the frantic mother. Again and again the cow flung herself against the grim sprawled shape, but the saurian with the wile of nearly a century in his cold reptilian brain was inexorable in his one-pointed objective.

At last, with but a few seconds between the little manatee and death, the most unexpected of allies joined in the hunt. Out from the nearby woods came the shabby figure of old Anse Wiatt, a bayou dweller who lived on a pine knoll a mile back from the lagoon. Anse was an old enemy of the manatees, but also of the tribe of 'gators. His shallow blue eyes had taken in the tableau with the instantaneousness of a camera lens, and with equal swiftness he made his decision. No humane impulse was back of it; manatees were simply everyday occurrences in the swamp, while a 'gator the size of this one was a rarity even in 'gator country.

Old Anse visioned that monstrous hide drying in his woodyard. The crack of his rifle shattered the silence of the cypress wood and his well-placed bullet entered the right eye of the saurian just as he was submerging. Stricken unto death he still hung at pause for the space of heavy mo-

ments it takes for the sluggish saurian brain to answer a
stimulus. Then his jaws gaped upon a rivulet of blood and
the giant bulk of him was lashing its life away in the shallows.

Meantime the little manatee, dazed and half strangled,
had been swept close beneath his mother's protecting flipper and convoyed to the cool darkness of one of their breathing caves beneath the bank. Once more, as if by the direct
intervention of fate, the little bull had been delivered from
death.

But not all his calfhood was composed of terror and
grim escapes. There were days of quiet and unbroken hap-
piness in the company of other calves, when he played,
quarreled, and basked in an Elysium of growing bliss. Sometimes two or three families would doze on the warm mud
flats while the little ones slid down the slippery banks to
land with a splash in the water, or sampled the tender water
grass in preparation for the vegetable diet that would soon
take the place of their mothers' milk.

Those were the days when the calf learned how to scratch
and curry his wrinkled skin by scraping and rolling over
on the gravelly stream bottoms, how to blow like his far-
off relative the whale by stretching apart his lip lobes and
spraying water in the air, how to sleep on the bottom of
deep pools for a half hour at a time by closing the stoppers
of his nostrils, and how to enjoy tender salads of water
sprouts. And all this time the growth of his body and the
craft of his small brain went on apace.

When the high water had gone and with it the saurian
invasion, the most dangerous period of the little one's calfhood came to an end. He was more than six months old
when one night, as the manatee family slept on the warm
clean sand with their tails in the water, the old leader of the

herd suddenly awoke. A distinct change was creeping through the waters of the lagoon. A shiver passed over him and immediately he went about waking his family. The first fall change had come, and from now on the water of the lagoon, which was affected by the ocean tides, would become colder. If the manatees did not hurry to the sheltered waters farther inland they would catch cold and die. They started at dawn, as fast as they could paddle toward the main river course, and then upstream toward a chain of shallow sequestered lagoons, where no coastal winds ever blew—the beginning of a hundred-mile journey to the herd's winter haven.

Sluggish swimmers at best, the herd of thirty-odd manatees covered little more than twenty miles a day, for they swam in straggling formation and stopped often to feed, foregathering only at night for mutual protection. Once in the dangerous river waters, small sharks and sawfish wandered in from the Gulf, haunted the depths, and the herd swam in protective formation, the females and young in the middle and a cordon of males on the outside, just as a herd of bison on land would move through enemy-haunted country.

The greatest joy the calf had yet known came with his first feel of the sweeping river current. New life and a fierce appetite rose within him, and his growth progressed at redoubled speed. When he lifted his head above the water, foam and spray blew into his face till he coughed and shook his head like a horse in strong oats. Down below he saw wonderful sights along the sandy bottom. Brown turtles and dark water snakes slipped swiftly along, hugging the banks, and schools of fish flashed everywhere about him. At night the herd slept on the sands at the stream's edge.

When they reached the remote network of waterways where the elders had spent a score of winters, they found many other families there before them. The woods round-about were like a vast still hothouse. Here the water growths were more luscious; man never penetrated here, for the region was a maze of swamps, tangled and shadowy even at midday. Overhead birds sailed and clamored.

The calf came to love the warm breathless nights when the big stars flamed like lamps strung among the high branches, making lanes of quicksilver and ink across the waters. He liked the dripping stillness, the occasional rains that flashed through the forest, and the swift salmon-colored dawns.

Now came the pairing time among the elders of the herd. For two weeks there was a foregathering of the many families at a still sandy bend of the river. All feeding stopped and the woods echoed to the short coughing snort of the big males and the splashing of many bodies. For the first time the calf was deserted by his mother and left in the company of calves of his own age.

These were pivotal days for him in which he learned his own strength and won easy ascendancy over the other yearlings of the herd. The youngsters had many a sham tussle and there was none who could hold his own against the young bull from Santee Lagoon. Quite automatically he took his place at the head of each foraging expedition.

With the coming of April the different families departed for their summer homes. The calf still swam close to his mother from force of habit, but their relationship was becoming negligible. She was already heavy with another calf and gave little thought to the bulky youngster who she knew would soon be seeking a mate of his own. Except for the larger sharks and alligators he now had no enemy to

fear save man. But against this last enemy, crueler than any
of the foes of sea, land or sky, he was to wage an unending
war until he died.

Men had become aware that the manatees in the vicinity
of Santee Lagoon were the last of their race in America. As
a result they were now a rarity for which many zoos and
museums were willing to pay big prices; and many a hunter
who had hitherto been oblivious of their existence now
wished to bag a specimen out of curiosity. The Government had placed a tardy penalty on every manatee killed,
but the prices offered by animal collectors were far greater
and there was little or no law enforcement in the sparsely
settled swamp country.

Gunners, white and black, took toll of the herd that
spring and it was then that the old leader of the Santee herd
fell to a Negro's bullet near the mouth of the home lagoon.
The herd flew asunder in panic, and it was not until evening, five hours later, that they reassembled, drawn by the
mysterious instinct of location all water dwellers have. In
the next few days four other members of the herd died,
having become entangled in cleverly laid nets.

Spring brought no peace to the manatee folk that year.
Week after week their numbers were being cut down.
Along all the miles of ponds and waterways there seemed
no yard of safety for the herd. Whenever they thrust their
whiskered masks above the water they caught the smell of
powder smoke or the death scent of human footprints along
the shore. Their only safety was in the depths of the lagoons
or the refuge caves beneath the banks.

Many of these caves had been discovered by crafty
woodsmen. Twice, followed by hunters in a bateau, and
agonized for rest and sleep, the calf sped for the underwater entrance to some cave, only to strike against the

strands of a net strung across the opening. Each time he had quickly been warned and backed out, escaping by the smallest margin. Instinct told him that no courage or cunning would avail long against man's relentless persecutions.

That fall the manatees gathered for their trip farther inland much earlier than usual, and from all the waterways there were no more than fifteen animals to make the passage after the ravages of the summer. By the time spring came again the dark-colored young bull swam at the head of the herd. He had attained a size greater for his years than that of any manatee the Florida lagoons had known for half a century. Huge of girth, he stretched a good twelve feet from nose to tail tip, and maturity would add another foot to that.

It was toward the end of that summer that Anse Wiatt, the piney woodsman, took note of the young bull and set himself the task of capturing him alive. Wiatt knew that this was the largest manatee that had ever lived in that region, and the fact opened several possibilities in his canny mind. Such a specimen would be a rarity anywhere. Few museums and scarcely a park or circus in the country held one of this vanishing tribe. Wiatt was already in touch with two animal collectors. If he could make his capture and dispose of the animal off Florida soil, the deal would net him close to a thousand dollars—quite a fortune among the pinewoods dwellers.

Braving the almost intolerable daytime heat of the lagoons, Wiatt prowled the waterways in his homemade canoe, sometimes drifting silently with the current, again ambushed for hours on some reedy bank. The longer he watched the more proof he got of the extra edge of cunning of the young bull who was now the actual king of all the sea cows in the region. Never did Wiatt get closer than two hundred yards from his quarry. He learned all the young bull's favorite basking places and again and again sighted him from some lookout tree, but always on approaching the spot he found that though other less wary animals were often still there, the monarch himself had slipped away, warned by the sagacity that had been ripening in him since calfhood.

Throughout the remainder of that summer Wiatt pitted his craft against the big bull and lost. But no animal can cope with man for long and win, for man has the faculty of infinite innovation. By the end of October, Wiatt devised an entirely new method for the capture of the young bull.

Having located all the breathing caves beneath the stream banks frequented by the bull and his followers he set cunning nets of line and wire at the entrance to each. Then he arranged for a manatee drive along the upper waterways with the aid of half a dozen Negroes who lived in the vicinity. Having first made sure that the big bull was feeding far up Cachet Creek, the drive was started upstream, the Negroes spread out in fan-shaped formation, two sculling in bateaus, the others wading alongshore in a hubbub of splashing and shouts. Every manatee in the small herd was started upstream ahead of the beaters, for noise filled them with panic. As Cachet Creek had no upper tributaries, Wiatt felt confident that it would be but a matter of hours before the prize was his. The shallow headwaters of the creek would be a cul-de-sac from which there was no way out except overland.

Throughout the long breathless afternoon the drive continued. But long before the fugitives reached the shallow waters of the creek the dark young bull sensed the trap in store. One by one he had sought the familiar refuge caves but sensed in time Wiatt's cunning snares. Sounding a water warning to the others of the herd, he turned and slipped silently back in the direction of the lagoons.

Swimming at top speed and close to the bottom he swept straight down upon his enemies. The creek was so narrow at this point that his bulk sent waves swishing up the banks and made his big glistening body look twice its normal size. The Negroes in their leaky bateaus uttered groans of superstitious terror as the gunmetal bulk of the bull surged past their crafts like a launched torpedo, and the barelegged beaters leaped up the banks.

Anse Wiatt, seeing what was happening from the back of his sorrel mare, yelled futile orders to the men, then, snatching up his rifle in a rage, sent a bullet after the disappearing bulk of the giant. By sheer luck his bullet entered the young bull's side and tore its way out at the base of the right flipper, half paralyzing his body.

That paralysis seemed likewise to affect his instinct and his sense of craft and caution, for on reaching the big lagoon he went lunging crazily about in great circles, driven on and on by his overwhelming pain. He continued to swim and swim for hours, senses blurred from suffering, only dully conscious of his surroundings, finding in his mighty expenditure of strength the one possible surcease from agony. He swam till the daylight died and the early moon poked up above the cypress spires, and finally his paroxysms began to lessen with his waning strength. After a time he simply floated on the surface of the blood-dyed water in exhaustion, still tortured, but no longer frenzied.

So it was that Anse Wiatt came upon him next morning, weak and feeble from loss of blood, too dulled to sense an enemy. Anse realized that the chance he had waited all summer had come at last. Whipped from coma by the scent of a human so close, the big bull tried to escape to deep water.

Wiatt blocked his way, shouting meanwhile till two of his Negro neighbors came running with ropes. A few minutes later the king of the lagoons lay helplessly bound in the shallows. All that evening Wiatt and the men worked at the construction of a raft which would convey him down-river to the Gulf.

The next afternoon at the river mouth off Charlotte Harbor, Wiatt's shady deal with the animal collector was completed. A small lugger which was to take the captive to New Orleans met the raft offshore; on her deck was a great tank of glass and metal in which these men had ordained that the manatee bull should languish for the remainder of his days. The captive, still trembling in every nerve from twelve hours of paralyzing fear and commotion, his hide parched and fever-dry from lack of water, presently found his lashings removed, while men fastened him into davit slings to be hoisted on deck. This completed Wiatt's part in the transaction, for man works only by adapting whatever end he has to his means.

But Nature, who adapts her many means to a hidden end, had a last word to say on the matter. Long ago she had conspired with the sun and the sea, the mother of all manatees. Time and salt water had weakened the rope and leather of the lugger's davit slings. Five feet in the air came a rending creak and a snap. Thirteen hundred pounds of hardened bone and muscle struck the plank raft with an impact that drove it half under water. Anse Wiatt was flung eight feet in the air from the upended platform. For a wild minute then, men shouted, sprang, and roared, but neither ropes nor human strength availed. With a seal-like roll and rush the bull manatee plunged into the cool green depths for which his whole being ached, and plunged bottomward.

For a moment the raft was pitched and tossed in a monster whirlpool. Then she slid clear and trouble ceased; all was quiet above water except for the vile human language that passed from man to man as each party laid blame on the other.

Down below in his watery habitat, the bull manatee was speeding heavily southward toward the safety of the tropical rivers of Mexico. Nor was he ever to lead his herd in the Florida lagoons again for that year marked the passing of his persecuted clan from United States soil. Neither Anse Wiatt nor the collector knew that their little conspiracy sounded the death knell to an epic, a million-year struggle for existence by one of the gentlest and most inoffensive of American animals.

▪ Flounder, Flounder in the Sea

IT WAS THE OCTOPUS WHO OWNED IT, THOUGH THE SAWFISH found it, and the flounder loved it. How many years it had lain there could not be said, but it must have been over 300. The octopus considered it his, no doubt, for he had lived by the rotting hull of the sunken galleon in which the treasure lay for more years than any of the weird dwellers of the deep-sea bottom could recall. He wasn't a real octopus, but a ten-armed decapod, or "kraken"; among the most awesome creatures left living on this earth.

The ship was one of the ancient treasure galleons of Spain. She had been wrecked far back in the days of the conquistadores, when homeward bound among the Carib islands. A spine of treacherous coral had slit her bottom open and she had sunk with all on board. For many years thereafter she had sailed the middle depths of the ocean, up and down the Gulf Stream, at that mysterious three-quarter-mile level at which wooden derelicts float until the petrifaction of the deep changes their water-soaked timbers to the consistency and weight of stone. Then she had slowly dropped until she found a final resting place on the broad ledge of an undersea volcano which towered up from the ocean floor.

Along the cliffs and terraces of the undersea mountain, a wondrous pageant of submarine life flowed and darted, drifted and came to rest. The upflung rampart of the mountain marked one wall of that mighty chasm through which the broad Gulf Stream is swung eastward from the Caribbean toward Florida; and up and down this warm, teeming current the mightiest and swiftest killers of the sea hunted singly and in packs, seeking what they could devour.

To devour—that was the primal urge of these shadow-haunted creatures. To devour, to breed, to escape their natural enemies; but first and last to devour—for all the salt-sea dwellers are driven by a voracity which no earthborn animal can know or compass. Many of the weird denizens were therefore equipped with such huge mouths that they were scarcely more than living funnels, constantly gaping at the large end; others had great membranous stomachs, flexible as rubber, and were capable of engulfing other fishes even larger than themselves.

As time went on the sunken wreck on the ledge sank lower into the mud and by degrees became a part of the color and contour of the mountainside. Her planks became furred with a coating of gray-green slime, the primal ooze from which all life sprang and to which all life finally returns.

Strange barnaclelike creatures attached themselves to her timbers; seaweed and waving turtle grass and clumps of purple and yellow sea cucumbers grew up around her and over her rotting decks, and long tangles of submarine grasses hung pendantlike from her dangling spars and broken masts. Some of them were like broad ribbons, and waved in the current above her deck like green pennants; others were like clusters of ticker tape flung over her decks and rails in some mute but gala celebration of a Wall Street canyon type; still others were like long gray matted beards.

In time her devastation was covered over by the clinging growths, and the ancient hull took on the appearance of a ship in full sail, slightly listing, as under the weight of canvas.

To the deep-sea dwellers who frequented those depths it was a fascinating and never-ending attraction. Through the gaping breaks in the shattered hull, when daytime changed the Stygian blackness of the depths to dull gray, a faint warm luster would show—the soft gleam of the raw, un-minted gold that still lay in jumbled piles within the galleon's hold. Some of it had tumbled out upon the ledge through the broken ribs and seams.

During all the unnumbered years since the gold had been stolen from the lordly Incas and the galleon had met her doom, that treasure was the one thing that had not changed—for gold, like true love, is inviolable and not to be corrupted. Not the slightest tarnish dulled the virgin metal, and strangely, the corroding moss and slime of the depths found no purchase on its smooth surface. Like all pure, rare things, the gold absorbed light; and year after year it continued to shed a faint glowworm luster of its own into those fear-haunted depths.

This glow, similar to the luminosity of many strange fishes of the sea bottom, was a ceaseless lure to all the dwellers roundabout. No fish swam by the ancient hull without pausing to gaze within at the magic gleam, and wonder; even passing sharks and the rorqual whale, one of the mightiest of living things, had paused and gazed and wondered at the unaccountable gleam that surrounded the sunken treasure. Eyes cold, flat, and cruel like deadly pale gems, eyes of awful and appalling blackness set in heads of horror, and eyes set on long waving stalks—all were drawn to the yawning gaps in the ship's hull to peer within at the filmy light.

Then certain swift assassins learned to utilize the fatal lure and took to lying in wait in the vicinity of the derelict to prey upon the curious. Chief among these was a huge sawfish with a fifteen-foot body of leaden gray, tipped with a shaftlike snout over four feet long, flat and tough as old ivory and studded above and below with keen, sawlike teeth.

For a year or more the sawfish haunted the wreck and waxed heavy and lazy on the easy killing among the credulous and curious, and came to look upon himself as the king of that particular neck of the sea. Only a few crabs were allowed to share the pirate's hunting ground—huge, hard-shelled, blood-red monsters of a size never seen in the upper waters.

But the reign of the sawfish was cut suddenly short. One day, as he lay in ambush, his cold, implacable eyes saw a terrible sight. Up along the slippery surface of the ledge, from the lightless depths below, a dead-white tapering tentacle protruded without warning. Yard after yard of it crept stealthily over the lip of the ledge like some great python, big around as a flagpole; and as if endowed with a brain and sentiency of its own, it investigated the wreck, feeling into all the holes and crannies.

An instant later a second tentacle followed it, and within a minute a mighty form of flabby flesh could be seen rising slowly from the depths. It was the kraken, the gigantic decapod which came from the uttermost depths at the ocean floor. The kraken's body alone was larger than the largest fish, its tentacles, radiating outward like the spokes of a wheel, were each nearly forty feet long, and covered with rows of round sucking disks, studded with fierce curved claws of black horn.

Intrigued by the feel of the derelict the monster rose to investigate. Like some gigantic bleached spider out of the realm of nightmare, he came climbing up the rocky slope. On the lip of the edge he poised for a space, staring with two great lidless eyes, set like pools of ink in the middle of his bulbous body. Long and long he stared, investigating every cranny of the sunken ship. Perhaps it was the gleam that drew him; at any rate, he stared and stared in strange fascination.

Then the sawfish performed an act of grim courage which must have gone far in balancing his long trail of crimes. His gray snout protruded stealthily from his ambush, took careful aim, then with a writhing flick of his steel-hard body he launched himself straight at the livid horror.

Swift as he was, the sentient arms of the bleached leviathan were swifter. Quick as the crack of a whip two unoccupied tentacles shot out and wrapped like living riatas of white gristle about the slate-gray body of the attacker.

It was a strange and fearful battle. Each of the contestants was the most awkward proposition the other had ever run into. Huge as the kraken was, and possessed of a stomach that was nothing more than a caldron of seething digestive juices, he was no sword swallower, and the sawfish, with his lean body composed of bone and leather, was little more than a nineteen-foot lance. Unable to engulf him, the decapod could but hold off and battle him against the rocks. But each time he was released the great sawfish came hurtling in again like a projectile. Once the kraken made the mistake of seizing the fish around his snout and had a tentacle lopped off. The decapod's ensuing rage was such that he flung his whole bulk upon the attacker and crushed him into the ooze. That time the sawfish's pig eyes were either blinded by the silt, or he had decided that discretion was the better part of valor; at any rate, he rushed out into the sea and never returned again.

Thereafter the kraken haunted the vicinity of the derelict and took up the sawfish's splendid system where the latter had left off. Even the colony of blood-red crabs soon disappeared down the new king's gullet. Only the voracious scavenger fish of the upper waters, which fed on floating fragments of battle that rose to the surface, could have begun to tell you the number and size of the slain who went to sate the unfillable maw of the monster during the many years that followed.

Naturally a dweller in the motionless cold and darkness of the sea bottom, the kraken in time wholly deserted his native haunts, to linger in the vicinity of the derelict, which exerted an irresistible influence over him. Possibly it was merely the realization of easy hunting that kept him there, but more likely it had something to do with the magic influence of the gold itself. Some wise man once wrote that of all living forms the octopus, with his clutching, indrawing arms, is the symbol of greed on this earth, and where there is gold treasure there greed abides.

There came at last a day of great change in the underwater world. A vast cataclysm in an adjacent part of the ocean bed had shouldered up a new range of submarine mountains and sunk another one; changing the currents as well as the temperature of the great ocean streams, filling the waters for miles around with a white calcareous ooze. Such a disturbance undersea is more drastic than the severest change of climate in the world above. This one was followed by a deathlike calm that pervaded even the upper reaches of the sea.

Up on the surface the water was as smooth as if it had been ironed out and Bill Newlin's small pearling lugger lay becalmed off Cat Island. As there was not even a puff of breeze to stir a sail, Newlin and his single diver, a Trinidad mulatto, sat fishing off the stern.

It was about midafternoon when Newlin began to notice a number of dead fish floating up to the surface—fish of weird and variegated forms such as were never seen in the upper ocean. For a space the two men sat in silence, considering the phenomenon while they smoked and watched their lines. Presently the Negro pointed a few yards to port.

"Look yonder, Cap'n," he said. "Dat a mighty big an' cur'ous kind of fish; queerest I ever see in dese waters. Sumpin' mighty funny must of happen down below, sah."

The floating mass at which he pointed was the mutilated remains of a ribbon fish of some ten feet in length, one of the strangest of the dwellers of the great depths, which flows through the water with a boneless oscillation like a long pennant waving in a breeze. Newlin brought the lugger closer and studied the body a minute in silence.

"You're right, Dirk," he answered. "There's been doings down below, and no mistake. A couple of mountains must have rose up and clapped together, or something. Here's hoping the reefs have juggled us a new deal. It's the only way we'll ever get a run of luck, maybe."

Dirk Henry, who had played Newlin's losing game with him for three years, grinned knowingly. "Dat bad luck can't hang on much longer, Cap'n, an' when she breaks she goin' break clean through. Dat the way it goin' be with us —she either all is or she all ain't."

A few minutes later the men hauled in their gill net and dumped its contents on the deck—three marble-green mackerel and another queer-looking gray-brown fish, round as a dollar, with a circular fin like a ruffle running round its flat body and two goggling, mild, inquisitive eyes. While the mackerel flapped and snapped with vicious force, the fourth fish lay still and seemed to gaze with mild reproach at the two men. The Negro sprang in and dispatched the mackerel with a club; then Newlin's voice stopped him short when his boot heel was raised above the fish of the round, goggling eyes.

"Hold on, Dirk! That fellow's no halibut, he's a deep-sea flounder. They're pretty hard eating, so there's no use killing him." He stooped over the queer round fish, which seemed to return his gaze inquiringly. "If I knew of a scientist hereabouts he'd pay me a good price for this fellow as a specimen that's mighty hard to catch, but I don't, so we may as well chuck him back." He picked the flounder up by its abbreviated tail and walked to the rail when an idea struck him. He grinned at Dirk: "This is the same kind of flounder those old boys back in the fairy tales wrote about. Remember how it went, Dirk? 'Flounder, flounder in the sea, see what you can do for me,' or some such thing. And then the fellow in the story chucked the flounder back, and right there his luck began. Maybe this one will bring something to us."

Dirk Henry, who had never read fairy tales, simply smiled tolerantly. He was used to the whims of his master. Newlin dropped the flounder overside. "So long, old-timer!" he called. "Remember us well to the clams and oysters, and if you got any pull, use it!"

The flounder sank quickly from sight. Down and down through the tranquil leek-green surface water he swam, toward the still depths from which he had come. He had experienced varied and direful terrors in the recent cataclysm of the sea bottom, but none so curdling as his brush with Bill Newlin. Still, he showed no sign of hurry in his wavering descent. He was never known to hurry. His was the peaceful nature of a philosopher.

This fish, less than three feet in diameter, was one of the two or three forms in all the ocean that possessed the open sesame of the two worlds of the sea; he was at home both at the surface and in the unplumbed depths. The flounder's secret was nothing more than that simple law of physics that water pressure is equal on all sides, and that water in itself is noncompressible. Therefore, as the flounder sank slowly downward he filled himself with water by degrees to meet his need, preserving a density equal to the medium through which he swam, as in the case with all bottom dwellers. Otherwise he would have been crushed to a mere fraction of his normal size.

Chance this day saw fit to lead the flounder's course toward the ledge where the sunken wreck lay, and an hour after Newlin had dropped him overside saw the fish settling contentedly in the ooze on the ledge, teeming with an abundance of the innocent fare on which flounders live—infinitesimal animal and vegetable particles, the curds and whey of deep-sea diet. Presently as he fed he was attracted by the faint soft shine that marked the location of the treasure ship. Flapping clumsily along the ledge, he moved forward to investigate. Long and long he stared with his dull, protruding eyes into the gaping breaks of the ship's side. Fortunately for him, the dread keeper of the treasure was at the time far distant.

All that day, following the great disturbance in the ocean bottom, a restlessness had been manifest in the lower depths.

It had affected even the mighty decapod, who, though he possessed nothing which could be tabulated as nerves, was stirred by a subtle unease as he noted the many fleets of bottom dwellers migrating upward out of the roiled waters below the ledge.

About midday there came to him one of those mysterious urges which the giant cuttlefish feel—a call to visit the upper reaches of the ocean for a brief period. So, launching himself from the ledge, he propelled himself upward in a series of swift backward lunges, by means of a powerful jet of water expelled from the saclike opening at the base of his tentacles.

It happened that about an hour after the catching of the flounder, Dirk Henry sat half dozing in the shadow of the deckhouse as he waited for a breeze.

All at once Dirk sat up with a galvanic start. A shiver of unaccountable dread had whipped him out of his doze, and he felt, even before he opened his eyes, the nearness of some sinister, watching presence. One glance overside, and with an inarticulate yell of terror he sprang toward the companionway. For, overside, the still surface of the sea was all awrithe with what seemed to Dirk to be a mass of great white snakes, and the humid air was filled with the sharp, strangling odor of musk, which hangs about the squib tribe like the carnal reek about the tigers of the jungle.

Bill Newlin, who came running up from below, found the Negro pointing overside, his face about three shades grayer than any mulatto's countenance has a right to be. For a while both men stood staring in speechless fascination. It was the first time either had ever glimpsed the mighty devilfish of the depths. Bill Newlin flung an arm up before his face with an involuntary cry of horror as, up from the center of the writhing mass of tentacles, rose the vast cylindrical body of the decapod—tons of livid flesh that reached almost as high as the lugger's scuppers. On top of this pallid mass two great lidless eyes now showed, staring straight at the ship with a malignancy that chilled the blood of the watching men. Beneath them gaped a cavern of a mouth that was overhung by a gnashing curved beak, horribly like that of a bird of prey.

Suddenly two white streamers shot out from this horrid tangle toward the ship's side and in another moment flowed up under the rail and along the deck. With a hoarse cry Newlin dashed into the cabin and brought back a repeating rifle. As quickly as he could aim and fire he sent three express bullets into the monster's flabby bulk, while Dirk, in a frenzy, sprang here and there hacking with a long knife at the clutching steamers that were licking in and out of the scuppers.

Every second the two expected to see the creature surge forward and overwhelm the small craft with his bulk. But even as they stood their ground, their teeth set, their breathing shaking their bodies in the stress of horror, the attack of the monster was suddenly withdrawn. A moment later the whole grisly bulk had sunk from sight, leaving the surface of the water again calm and unbroken. Only a bleached fragment or two of the tentacles that lay on the deck remained to prove that the kraken had not been a ghastly apparition.

"God!" breathed Newlin, wiping the clammy sweat from his brow with his shirt sleeve. "Is that the kind of luck that flounder brought us? What next?"

As he spoke a sudden flap of canvas signaled the first of the rising breeze and the sails which had been hanging limply bellied half-full. All afternoon the storm that had been brewing had edged around to the south. In the next ten minutes the wind rose in gusts, accompanied by the rumble of thunder. Without words—for both men were shaken to the core by their recent experience—Newlin and Dirk hurriedly shortened sail and ran for the shelter of the island, to spend the night ashore.

Meanwhile the devilfish was shooting downward again, leaving behind him a stream of the pallid fluid which answered for blood for such as he. His wounds, though not fatal, were painful in the extreme, and had aroused in him the most terrible rage he had ever known, for he had developed through the years the testiness of a despot. Unerringly he returned through the pathless wilderness of waters to his favorite haunts upon the submarine mountain ledge, guided by that marvelous inner compass all seafolk have to a sublimated degree.

As he went, news that the mighty king of the depths was wounded went abroad in some mysterious way, and soon there were lined up in his wake some six or eight fierce pirates of the shark clan—the wolves of the sea. As yet they did not dare to attack, but none knew better than they the almost inevitable finish that must overtake the weakened or wounded in the lower depths.

Not long after the flounder had settled in the mud beside the wreck, his subtle sense of danger signaled warning to his efficient little brain, and while his nearsighted eyes had yet seen nothing, that instinct caused him to dart with a quick wriggle within the hull of the derelict, leaving only a thin line of bubbles in his wake. He was but a foot in advance of a swift tentacle which came shooting along the ledge from behind a huge thicket of spongelike growth thirty feet away. The decapod had returned stealthily as a great spider, after the manner of his kind.

No sooner was he within the darkness of the ship's hull,

however, than the flounder executed another move, probably the quickest of his life, for out of the shadows death came toward him, the most sinister kind of death that lurks upon the ocean floor.

To look at, the stranger was neither swift nor menacing, yet this small, undelineated creature, something like a three-foot length of bologna sausage, was an enemy more to be dreaded than a crew of tiger sharks. His name was *Simenchelys parasiticus*, and he was the most deadly of the tribe of boring eels.

Monsters that could have swallowed a dozen of him at a gulp fled at his approach, for wherever the diminutive mouth of the *Simenchelys* fastened itself, death was the result. Once his head clamped fast to his victim, nothing short of amputation of the part would release him, while the amazing tongue of the *Simenchelys*, long and sharp as a keyhole saw, cut through flesh and bone like a dentist's drill, until within a few brief minutes the whole body of this sea leech was embedded in his victim, there to remain boring and feeding on his living prey until nothing remained but a lifeless husk. So highly specialized in destruction was he that his body could be cut in two, and the anterior end would go on in its terrible devouring, healing as it went.

Roused from his haunts at the sea bottom, the *Simenchelys* had come swimming up the ledge and taken refuge in the sunken wreck while the decapod was absent. And thus it was he, instead of the flounder, which the questing feeler of the monster contacted inside the darkened hull.

Rage and pain must have robbed the kraken of all sense of caution, for without mangling his victim he sucked the eel into his maw. In an instant he rued it. With a writhing heave his great bulk was off the ledge and the kraken was clawing at his open mouth with three of his arms, and ejecting fierce streams of water. Of no avail were his titanic struggles, for the nemesis within him was already at work.

Now the waiting shark folk, which had followed the kraken from the upper waters, began edging in. Their cold little eyes had seen what had happened—it was as if from the beginning they had known the end. Now they spread out in a circle and began venturing rushes with the same deadly pack unity of the wolves of the upper world.

The battle that followed was fierce and grim. The kraken though he knew he was doomed, preserved his arrogant sovereignty to the end, forcing the offensive. But the outcome was never once in the balance, for other monsters had been drawn by the silt clouds which rose like smoke from the scene of the struggle—terrible pikelike creatures with crocodile jaws, large as the largest sharks.

From the dimness within the galleon's hull the dull eyes of the flounder watched the long battle until the ship herself was torn loose from the ledge by the kraken's dying convulsions.

Meanwhile the storm that had broken the night before was the kind that often follows a great seismic disturbance. For three days and nights a hurricane such as had not been known in the Caribbees for a decade unleashed itself from the south, until all the smaller coral islands were awash, and the surface of the sea was plowed to an unusual depth. For the first time in many years surface dwellers were driven to seek quiet in the depths.

It was the height of this storm which marked the passing of the king of the devilfish. It marked also the passing of the sunken galleon, for at the end of the third day, when the tortured waters stilled, the ghost-gray ship with her luring gleam no longer stood upon the ledge.

That morning Bill Newlin, walking along the island

beach as he waited for the sea to subside, blundered on the first bit of luck he had known in his diving career. The whole shore line had been changed and inundated by the storm, and as Newlin moved along the tide line he stubbed his bare toe on a queer-looking piece of rock half buried in the sand. Something made him examine the object more closely and he rose after a moment with a smothered whoop of amazement.

In his hand was a small lump of the raw gold which had lain so many years in the wrecked galleon's hold. The sunken ledge on which the ship had lain so long was but a continuation of the shelving spine of land of which Cat Island formed the highest peak. During the hurricane the ancient wreck had been broken to pieces, and this trace of its precious treasure had been swept ashore by the pounding seas.

Skilled in deducing such signs, Newlin needed no further clue. That afternoon found him and Dirk Henry sounding along the sunken ledge and, judging keenly the set of tide and current, their eyes lit with that mirrored glow which buried treasure alone can bring to the faces of men. Before nightfall they had solved the secret of the sunken ledge, and the diving had begun.

Within a week the undersea mountain had yielded up a golden harvest. On the proceeds of it Bill Newlin sailed shortly for the North, a rich man. To Dirk Henry fell the old lugger and some twenty-five hundred American dollars, a sum which stood for a vast fortune in the Caribbees. He is still a colored Croesus of his native island.

▪ Seekonk, the Tale of a Sea Gull

No one knew in just what noisesome rookery of thieves, on what rocky island or robber's cove the old grizzled white gull was reared, not even old Gadgett, the lightkeeper. But there were many middle-aged men around Kittery Harbor who could not remember a time when the old pirate had not wheeled and screamed above the gray-green waters of the bay. If the facts were known, old Seekonk had doubtless been a grown bird when they were boys, for ornithologists tell us that the lifetime of many of his clan is close to a hundred years.

Ancient he was, beyond question. You could tell it by his eye as he would float past you, insolently close, turning his head to gaze—an old eye, wise, canny, tyrannous with authority. His plumage showed it, too, by its rough and molting look, and the leprous white splotches on the gray of his mantle. But most of all you could tell by the voice, which cracks with age in a gull as it does in a human. On cloudy days when the flock circled high in the mists with the wild, strident "S-e-i-o-u! S-e-i-o-u!" that is the sea gull's storm signal, you could pick out old Seekonk by his deeper note which broke in the middle and ended in a bass "konk" like a Canada goose. It was this that gave him his name.

For years he was known about the harbor by his great size, for he was larger than any other gull of the flock by nearly two inches. But through the latter years of his life, after the snow of his plumage had lost the sleek sheen of condition, he was known chiefly through the loss of one leg, doubtless parted with in the jaws of some ravenous young shark.

That day had marked the beginning of his downfall. For many years he had been by way of being the monarch of the Kittery beaches. Gull flocks have no actual authoritative leaders, but Seekonk had been one of the chief leading spirits of the yelping and rascally crew of a hundred-odd gulls to which he belonged. He did not pretend to command, but he knew, and his many relatives in the raucous gang knew, that the flock fattened on Seekonk's wit and daring.

There was nothing in aerial lore he did not know. He was loudest of voice, foremost in cunning and impudence; above all others he could usurp the choicest fishing ground, or dare to drop a fat fresh clam from far aloft onto the hard-packed sand of the beach to break its shell, without fear of its being purloined by any of his thieving kindred, because he had the bulk and the strength and the pickax beak to back his daring.

But all that changed on the day he came winging in from some deepwater fishing with a bleeding stump where one leg had been. And the first thing he did on landing was to take a nose dive on his beak in the soft sand of the beach that had been his kingdom. He had lost the fine finesse of balance and control; he was no longer a master wingman.

Perhaps like Caesar landing in Egypt he saw in that spill a symbol of his downfall, but he failed to carry it off with a "by this sign I conquer thee, O Egypt." Being a bird he was stricken, and so he huddled the rest of the day by himself, taking no part in the raucous yelp and skirmish of the flocks as they filled their gullets at the tide line. And later when they all eddied and funneled in the last of the sunset light, talking noisily over the luck and excitement of the day, Seekonk took no part in the clamor, nor did he follow them that night to the rookery on the rocky islet in the bay. His leg stump was a stiff and fevered torment; all that night he huddled miserably on the sand, stricken to the depths of his grim bird heart. His hard eyes blinked impenetrably and told no tale, but his draggled wings hung in the sand and spelled utter dejection.

Next morning the flock came wheeling back in a screaming cloud and settled with calls and chatter on the beach. They flapped and preened and the early sun glinted on their sleek livery. Did they take note of Seekonk and his plight? Good heavens, they had talked of little else through the night—cruel, shameless, heartless intrigue, as all gull gossip is. They huddled in dense ranks close by, but not too close, and sized up his plight with inimical eyes that seemed looking at nothing in particular. And anon they sailed above him in a ragged storm to eye him from aloft, with mewings and chuckling twitters that might have passed for dry mirth. But that was the extent of things for the time being, for Seekonk's had been the strong beak among them and all was not certain yet.

But at sunset when he roused himself and made shift to feed with them at the tide line—that was pitiful. He hopped drunkenly on his one leg, balancing with spread wings, and in the first snatch for a sand crab, pitched miserably on his beak before all the watching crew. Twice a slapping wave knocked him sprawling, left him flapping in the back-wash. Within ten minutes three or four of the bolder spirits were snatching up choice morsels within six inches of his outstretched beak with yelps of glee, cruel as he had ever been in the arrogance of his strength. His downfall was complete.

How the mob savored it! They made a very circus among themselves. They swooped down, veered and volpaned above him, screaming as if to say: "Look at him! Look at him now! A cripple! A one-legged cripple! S-e-i-o-u! S-e-i-o-u! He couldn't hurt a sandpiper. Ha, ha, ha, ha, ha!"

Bold and brazen they were in their mob solidarity. Even the low characters of the beaches were there—the mere riff-raff and hangers-on of the flock—the down-at-the-heels, out-of-work and decrepit, and they did not stop at jibes and jeers, for all had a bone to pick with the fallen one. Even his mate was among them—she, too, had turned. That was but true gull nature. No love lost there, however. Theirs had been but a partnership of conspiracy and sordid necessity at best; never a day but the pair had fallen out two or three times at least, yelling and pecking at one another till the female went off to sulk on the sand.

Never a time when either would not have snatched the choicest fish from the other's very beak, or desert him cold at threat of danger. But what more could be expected in a tribe whose very young have neither care nor recognition for their parents, and who are often pecked to death by the old birds for wandering into a strange nest. Robber law is fine enough for the strongest of the fit, but for the weak and the maimed it holds neither ruth nor pity. That night on the rock islet where the flock slept, Seekonk sulked wretched and alone on a high rock. He was sick, sick to the heart, of the bullying and belittlement he had endured, and sore from his fevered leg. There is nothing quite so desolate as a flock bird alone and in pain, but Seekonk was merely taking the bitter pill he had made for himself during years of rascally life. His knack of patience, of deathless persistence which the sea had taught him must serve him now, for this he had, as the very sands of the beaches where he lived.

Next morning in the chill before the sun, Seekonk with a stiff rustle of harsh loose feathers spread his wings and beat in to shore, hoping to elude the belittlement of his fellows in some quiet place till his pain and fever ceased. But no.

Within the hour the far calls of the harpy crew came faintly down the wind as they sought their breakfast along the shore. They sought also old Seekonk and presently found him at the edge of the dunes, where he sat still and white as a gravestone, head sunk on his breast. An inquisitive head set with two eyes like crumbs of black glass presently spied him out and yelled the news, and down came the straggling throng again, wheeling and screaming. And old Seekonk lifted the film of exhaustion he had let slip over his black eyes and braced himself to take it.

A gull flock constitutes one of the grimmest of all schools of life and death. As one naturalist has said, "The rapacity of the birds begins where that of the mammal leaves off." That day was even worse than the preceding one for the old gull. He paid for every piece of highbinding he had ever perpetrated, with interest compounded by the hour. The crowd was bolder now; they jibed and yelped abuse; at feeding time they snatched food from beneath his very beak, and made bold to jostle him—but from behind. None cared even now to clash with him head on, for that javelin bill was still on duty.

For more than a week the game went on. Then gradually the flock tired of their fun, even as alley brats tire of deviltry, and the crueler game began, the slow process of elimination, of ostracism and utter disregard. His fellow fiends, beside filching from him unmercifully, ignored him completely, turned their backs and went on about flock affairs as if he were not there. He who had been the wiliest and strongest of the lot gradually fell to the position of camp follower and hanger-on. Each day he flew to and from the island with the flock, but he sat and fed always a bit apart, always in the wake, for fear of being knocked over and trampled. Everyone has seen something of this stage of an old gull's freeze-out. Hardly a gull flock but has one or two ill-conditioned or crippled members who suffer the wholesale insult of the mob.

Why didn't he take himself off, and be done with the humility of it? He had tried it, heaven knew, but it didn't work, for he was a shore bird, and all shore birds simply have to hobnob with someone, if only the pipers who trip along the sand, like marbles rolling just beyond the lap of the waves.

For a day he would sit apart, gnawed by the incurable gregariousness of his kind, but always the empty loneliness would be too much; the far cries of the happy, talking flock, the echo of their whimpering wings pulled like unseen cords at his breast. They told him that alone he was nothing, a mere fraction, an aliquot part of the grim group entity with which he had flown.

What was that wild jubilance that came to him down the wind? Perhaps they had found a dead leviathan, stranded and well-ripened under the burning sun; or picnic refuse left by humans on the sand. He must see, he must see. At first only his wings would flutter and spread involuntarily, and his neck began to crane, but finally swamped in a fierce inquisitive wave, he would flap aloft and sail away to seek reunion with what can only be termed the spirit of the flock.

Spring passed and summer drew on, bringing close the nesting time of the sea birds. The harbor became filled with the thin wild dirge of hundreds of stranger gulls come up from the south on the first lap of a journey that would end on some rock-girt shore up near the Arctic Sea—the secret unknown which man has rarely seen, where the great gull tribe repairs to rear its young, and in cases, to find new mates.

For a week the furor and excitement lasted; then one day the great conglomerate flock that peopled the harbor reaches, felt simultaneously the first definite summons of the far northern summer, and with many rally calls, all rose funneling into the blue and decamped toward the north. With them went old Seekonk, simply because he had to. No mate now took the journey with him; no eggs or fledglings would be his at the end of that long traverse, yet nothing but death could have kept him back. He flew as of old, as if wired to his place in the ragged flock formation.

They made the flight in short erratic jumps, after the manner of gulls. There was little order in their ranks, they spread out in a tattered cloud, flying low on the lookout for plunder. Once they followed in the wake of a big liner for two days, squabbling as they fattened on the waste dumped overside, for they are the original "white wings" of the world.

At the end of two weeks they arrived at their goal, the desolate rocky cliffs to the north of Hudson Bay, where millions of wild fowl of every tribe and land disappear each year to nest during the short Arctic summer. The gulls returned to the stretch of rocky beach on which they had reared their young for unnumbered years in the past. Thousands of other birds had arrived before them from the southland; sea and sky were filled with their legions, for the far-flung domain was one of the few places where man, the greatest and the cruelest of all enemies, never stalked.

It was not long before old Seekonk rued the urge that had brought him north. For here not only the songsters and shore birds, but many of the fiercest killers of the sky, resorted each year to prey upon the young and the unfit— great chocolate-colored sea eagles, fierce falcons, and goshawks. These air kings, however, did not deign to trouble themselves over a crippled gull, with the pick of thousands of tender duck and geese at their disposal. It was from his own tribe that Seekonk now came to be harried in a crueler way than he had ever known in the south.

Great black-backed and ivory gulls, with a wingspread of over five feet, attacked him daily, buffeting and robbing him without mercy. On the wing he could still hold his own with any of his tribe, but on the shore, in alighting or taking off, he was at the mercy of the many footpads of the beaches. All of these—the swift skuas, the jaegers, who are the hawks of the sea, and the ill-named laughing gulls—had taken note of his weakness, for all lived by holdup.

He made up somewhat for this, however, by pilfering in his turn from the pelicans as all gulls do. Master fishermen though they were, these great birds had no fight in them and little wit, so that even a lame gull could rob them with impunity.

The swift wonder of the northern summer came to an end. Seekonk had looked on detached and inimical, while his erstwhile spouse, now allied with an old enemy of his, had brought forth a nestful of scrawny brats. He knew the lady well, to well, in fact, and knowing, felt no loss. Sometimes, indeed, when he heard her harsh vitriolic voice raised in a squabble, he was glad to be quits.

By the time September came and the young fledglings of that year were able to fly, the flock took off again for the south. Seekonk went with them and was almost happy for the few fleeting days of the passage, for in the air he seemed wholly one of them again, his weakness quite concealed. Fierce, taciturn, bitter at heart though he was, he was nevertheless among the largest and handsomest members of the great flock when the birds were on the wing.

Wild things gain wisdom in three ways: through experience; through drawing on the massed experience of their kind, which is instinct; and in rare cases, through contact with man. Through chance and his disablement Seekonk came in time to tap this last and greatest source of cunning.

Back once more on the old Kittery beaches he made use of much he had learned in the north, but the foolish pelicans did not frequent those shores and he was cut off from his easiest source of revenue. But that year people took special note of the one-legged gull who was jostled by his fellows and had to take the leftover feeding along the shore. Many came to know him like an old friend, and now a few took pity on him and brought scraps of food to the beach. Though he could not know it, he had attracted the notice of some learned men and figured in a write-up in an ornithological paper.

The seasons slipped by. In spring and fall Seekonk continued to haunt the Kittery beaches, moving southward down the coast in midwinter. In summer the myriad flocks of the far north knew him again. Each year he made the long migrations with his fellows, not through love, but because he had to, being in spite of all a mere unit in the collective group soul of his band.

But there came a year at last when encroaching age and disability prevented his taking off when the flock went winging northward for the nesting. A few days before, a passing goshawk had disputed with him over a fat fish and left him with a fractured wing. Frantically, with hoarse wild cries he struggled to beat upward in the wake of the flock as it sailed away up the bay, but his injured wing tilted him far to one side and back he sagged to earth again, to go flapping and stumbling miserably along the beach, part leaping, part skimming, part hopping—a grotesque nightmare of a dance on his one leg—somehow, anyhow to follow on in the wake of the disappearing flock. He covered miles that way along the shore, till the glinting flock quite vanished on the far horizon, leaving him pitched forward on his breast in the sand, like a wrecked plane, head still strained upward, heart shaking his body and pounding as if it would blow up.

The loneliness he then knew was the most terrible he had yet suffered. It was tragedy, the wrench of which no human could quite comprehend. The empty desolate beaches, the silence and the lonely nights. For days he flapped up and down the shores calling out to the waves and the sky, complaining to any who cared to hear in the immense empty spaces, of his misery. For on top of all this his feeding was likewise impaired, for it takes a fine wingman to pounce on a fish as it flashes momentarily beneath the surface of the water. He fell to beachcombing, subsisting upon the inconsequential whatnot the waves washed up on the shore, and sand crabs, of course.

It was about this time that he made by chance his lasting

acquaintance with old Gadgett, keeper of the Kittery light-house that stood on a rocky point of land at the harbor mouth. Gadgett had studied gull ways and flight at closer range for more years than any other man in the region, for there was little else to occupy his days. In fact, he already knew old Seekonk, had marked him long ago from among his fellows, and watched the different stages of his down-fall.

One day as the old gull went flapping and hopping along the shore, uttering his lonely dirge, his course led him out on the rocky spit of land on which the light stood. And presently as he hopped painfully about, calling and peering among the rocks, he suddenly stiffened to attention.

"S-e-i-o-u!" The call came from hard by in quick answer to his own. It was so close, and so startlingly and indubitably a herring gull's call that Seekonk jumped. Cocking his head he saw the light tower standing near. Above the open door on a perch that stuck out from the wall sat a fierce-looking green-feathered bird with hard yellow eyes and a curved beak. It was he who had uttered the call, certainly a friendly thing to do in one who talked an alien tongue. Seekonk answered him with a soft yodeling note of pleasure, and cocking his head wisely, the other bird repeated the cry, loud and raucously as if insanely pleased with the effect, hitching up and down on his perch. The voice had a break in it, for he, too, was an old bird, old as Seekonk himself, and doubtless lonely.

Then something fell close to Seekonk's foot. He saw it was a piece of bread. Then he spied old Gadgett, the light-keeper, sitting just inside the open door, watching him. With swift hammerlike blows of his beak, Seekonk pecked and snatched at the bread, fearful lest the other bird would come and rob him, but the green one never stirred, simply watched like his master, with an air of patronage, while the hungry old gull fed.

Seekonk finally flapped away, but he returned thereafter every day, and hopped near the green bird who could always be relied upon to be sitting on the sunny side of the light tower of an afternoon. Always scraps of food were thrown to the visitor by the old lightkeeper who watched curiously from his window. The green bird, a parrot, of course, was a pleasant yet disconcerting sort of companion, wrapped up in his own noise and posturings. His huge, hooked beak which looked so formidable, was really only a caricature, for by nature he was giddy and quite harmless.

In time the two old birds came to sit quite close together in the misty light of afternoon.

The weeks passed and Seekonk's heart became filled with a new peace. The green parrot was different from all other birds, and old Gadgett seemed different from all other men. Seekonk lost his harsh suspicion, the overwhelming fear that keeps all wild things at bay, makes them hunted creatures outside man's pale. For the first time in his grim existence food was always forthcoming, always plentiful, and he did not have to fight and fend for every mouthful. In time he came to eat with a certain grace, forgetting to bolt.

Then the gull flock came winging back again, and for a time Seekonk came no more to the light. But the injury to his wing was a permanent one, and that fall saw him deserted once again, wandering the empty beaches, more desolate, more bitter than ever. No more for him were the long happy flights with his kind, and the joy and exhilaration of new sights and feeding.

November saw even the geese and swans sweeping southward, fleeing the Arctic. Only Seekonk remained, wandering the empty shores. Ice tinkled now around the salt marshes, and the harsh grasses grew brittle and rimmed with hoarfrost. Seekonk came again to the light, but though he hopped and circled on the rocks, there came no answer to his call. The ancient parrot had succumbed to a final illness with the first of the cold weather.

Old Gadgett laid out food, and on the day when the first flakes of snow rode the stinging wind, he caught the old gull and took him in. Thereafter Seekonk occupied the green one's cage in the light tower, and was fed often and well in a metal cup, but it was not the same. He sat hunched up all day in the corner, wings drooping, as one lost in memories, shutting himself away behind the film which covered his hard old eyes.

Long before the spring winds blew again, old Gadgett found him one morning, cold and stiff in the cage corner. No need to ask of what he had died. He had learned of gentler, finer ways than sea gulls ever dreamed, yet it was sheer pining that killed him—a loneliness for the cruel and rowdy rabble of the flock.

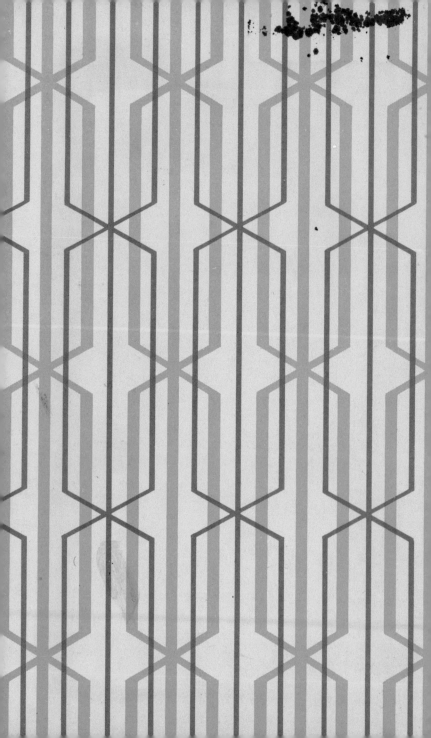